FOR THE SAKE OF LOVE

FOR THE SAKE OF LOVE

Chrissie Loveday

CHIVERS

British Library Cataloguing in Publication Data available

This Large Print edition published by AudioGO Ltd, Bath, 2011.
Published by arrangement with the Author.

U.K. Hardcover ISBN 978 1 408 49317 5
U.K. Softcover ISBN 978 1 408 49318 2

Printed and bound in Great Britain by
CPI Antony Rowe, Chippenham and Eastbourne

PROLOGUE

Amanda Jayne Manon stared dejectedly through the window of her small flat. She stroked her swollen belly and sadly twisted the wedding ring from her finger. 'Hello baby,' she muttered, as she did at least once every hour or more. 'I'm trying very hard to do my best for you but it's so tough. Okay, I know it's all my fault that you won't have a daddy to love you but maybe I can love you enough for the two of us. Whatever the world says about me, I'll always know I did the right thing at the time. I love you, baby.'

She sighed deeply. There were still seven weeks to go before the birth and she needed to make her final plans. She wouldn't be able to work for much longer.

'This magazine job is much too stressful for you and baby,' the midwife had told her, as she neared her time. Besides, she felt distinctly unwell and needed some rest, Her editor, the oh-so-perfect Penelope Withenshaw, had been unsympathetic.

'Of course you're entitled to maternity leave, darling,' she'd said in a tone that had disapproval dripping from it. 'Just make sure you're back in the fold preferably within days. If you're to be of any use at all, you need to be able to whizz off anywhere at a moment's notice.'

'But Penelope,' she began.

'Don't have "but" in my vocabulary. Of course, if it's a problem . . .'

The woman had no heart. Or understanding. She who knew nothing about children. Not that Amanda knew much but the learning curve was steep and fast.

'I'll do my best to find adequate child care.'

'Adequate doesn't come near, darling. Get it sorted or I'll have to appoint one of the many dozens of girls just waiting in the wings.'

Where on earth would she find the sort of childcare that Penelope was demanding? Did it even exist and if it did, how could she afford it? Would she be happy with someone else bringing up her precious baby? Her future as a single parent was beginning to look bleaker by the minute. Ingenuously, she had believed she would be able to work from home and send in her material from there. Penelope would not hear of it. Her editor sat in her large air-conditioned office, immaculate as ever and quite implacable.

'You need to be here. On the ball. Ready to follow up leads and catch the celebs when and wherever they are. If you don't want to do the job . . .'

'Of course I want the job. I love it and I'm good at it.'

'Yes, I'll grant you that. You certainly have the knack of getting close and asking the right questions. But just lately, you're letting this . . . this pregnancy,' said with a sneer, 'become the most important thing in your mind.' Of course this baby was filling Amanda's mind!

Did Penelope totally live and breathe her magazine, *Personal*, Amanda wondered? It seemed to be the only family, lover, life she needed. Nobody had ever heard her speak of anything or anyone else in her life. She was never seen without perfect makeup and elegant clothes, she was totally chic. Amanda felt positively frumpy, despite the most stylish maternity clothes she could lay her hands on. Her complexion and hair looked good, she knew, but there still remained the ever increasing middle section.

Everything was different for her now. She'd been willing to devote her own life to the magazine and rising to one of the senior reporters over several years. Until she had met Sacha. To say she'd been swept off her feet by the handsome tennis player was a total understatement.

CHAPTER ONE

How long ago did it all begin? Amanda scarcely remembered. Penelope had demanded that she should get an interview with 'someone significant in tennis'. The grass court season was just beginning to get started and so it was current and newsworthy. She wanted to get the low down on one of the major tennis hunks who were in Town. Precisely as instructed, the keen reporter had hung around outside the courts and managed to waylay Sacha after his defeat at one of the lesser tournaments. She'd picked up the information on the match as the supporters left the courts. He'd been expected to win but was having a bad day. At first, he'd waved her aside, clearly battered by his loss.

His perfect English, spoken with a hint of a French accent was enough to make her feel weak at the knees. Weak didn't even come close. She looked up at him, towering over her with his six feet four of muscular body, as perfect a specimen of manhood as she could ever hope to see, let alone be as close as this. Despite his obvious rejection, her years of practice made her persist in her quest.

'I'm so sorry. I know the last thing you want to do is talk about losing but I promise you, have a drink with me and I won't even mention

1

the subject.'

'Have a drink with you? Why on earth should I?'

Not my best interview opening, she thought. But necessary for her job.

'Sorry. You just looked so deflated. I felt so sorry for you. I know what it's like to have the sort of day that makes you wish you'd never got out of bed. Not even cappuccino with chocolate sprinkles and an oversized double chocolate muffin can do it for me. But . . . I bet you never eat such junk food.' His eyes held a glimmer of a smile and the corners of his mouth were twitching slightly.

'Now what makes you think that? Carbs are always important and with added chocolate, what could be nicer?' When he said chocolate, he pronounced it with a 'sh' sound and even added the final 'e' as a separate syllable. It sounded incredibly sexy. She would always call it shocolatay from this moment on.

'Okay. So, where do you suggest we go for this drink?'

'Oh wow. You mean you will? Right, that's wonderful.' She needed to think fast before he had the chance to change his mind. 'Okay. Okay. I have my car parked near here. We can go to a wine bar. Or somewhere else if you prefer. Do you drink? Maybe you don't drink alcohol with your training schedule. So maybe it should be a coffee house.' She was babbling. 'Sorry. This is exciting for me, though. You're my first tennis star.'

'I'm not sure what you mean. Your first?'

'Oh, sorry. I mean . . . I'm such a fan. Of tennis. Of you.' She did not want to give away the fact that she was seeking an interview. Not yet. She needed to get him into her car before she let that little nugget slip. 'I mean, I've been a fan for years. Tennis that is. I haven't ever talked to anyone involved before. Not a famous player.'

'I'm hardly famous. Yet,' he added with a grin. 'I do intend to play all the big tournaments though. Maybe that makes me start to be famous. In France, I am well known. Okay. So where is this coffee bar with the triple chocolate muffins?'

'Double. Double chocolate. Not far.' They reached her small car and he dumped his oversized tennis bag in the back, almost filling the entire rear seat. 'Excuse me asking, but how were you proposing to get back home? You could hardly walk far with that lot.'

'My coach was organising a cab for me. He'll be absolutely furious that I have left, of course. Probably write me off completely, after today's disaster,' he added gloomily.

'I'm sorry. I'd hate for you to be in any trouble on my account.' He folded himself into what was clearly an inadequate sized car seat for him and they drove off.

'Don't worry. My trouble is all of my own doing. This is a pleasant relief from the

3

pressures. There's always someone pestering me outside the courts. Fredo, my coach, guard dog, mother substitute and publicity agent, usually protects me from anyone and everyone. Interviews, radio, television, magazines. They want to know everything about me for some reason. So intrusive.' Amanda blanched. She was yet another of these tiresome people. 'Even the most intimate details,' he went on. 'I guess they practically want to know how many times I sneeze in a day. I just hate gossip writers.'

She giggled nervously. At what point did she have to confess the truth? He'd just described her job exactly. For once, she could see the other side of it. Always, she'd told herself it went with the territory of fame: the gossip columns and true life stories. If she confessed the truth right now, that would be it. No more talking of any sort. And she knew she could listen to him talk all day. That accent was incredibly attractive, even though his English was so perfect. Her heart was making the sort of gyrations she hadn't remembered existing for some months. She swallowed hard and grabbed her senses back into some sort of order.

'You speak such good English. Where did you learn?'

'My father is British. My mother is French. We have a family business down in Provence. We mostly lived in France or Spain. Tennis coaching is better there. I played from an early age but only became a professional in recent years. I've won a number of tournaments but I think I may have left it too late to be really successful. These are the times of the tennis teenager. I'm already twenty-five but, I reckon I'm as fit as most on the circuit.'

'Oh, yes. I'd certainly agree with that. You're as fit as anyone I know.' She grinned, wondering if he was aware of the double meaning in today's slang. She drove carefully, hoping the nearest coffee place would have somewhere to park.

'You are such a pleasure to speak to,' Sacha told her after they'd spent almost two hours over coffee. 'No hang-ups. No ulterior motives. I'd like us to share some more time together. I so rarely meet normal, happy girls. Your beauty adds even more to my pleasure. Now my part in this tournament is over, I can relax for a while. You can be my compensation. Will you have dinner with me?'

'I'd love to,' she replied, her eyes already bright with anticipation. Somehow, she'd forgotten all about the article she was supposed to be researching. She'd simply tell Penelope that she'd been unable to find anyone to talk to. Dinner with this gorgeous man who gave a wonderful French lilt to every word he spoke, how could she possibly say no?

'So. You will kindly return me to my apartment and then we can meet again in a short while. I need to shower and change my clothes. Do you know somewhere good to eat?'

'Of course. What sort of food do you want?'

'Italian, preferably. Though anywhere will be a pleasure with you accompanying me.'

'I bet you say that to all the girls.' *What a smoothie*, she told herself but it was still lovely to be spoken to like that.

'Hey . . . no. What do you take me for?'

'Well, a good looking man who probably has his choice of all the women he could wish for.'

'Not true. I'm usually guarded within an inch of my life. Fredo is like one of those large guard dogs. Rottweilers, are they called? He rarely lets me out of his sight. I'll be lucky to get out this evening without him insisting on joining us.' Her face dropped with disappointment. 'Don't worry, cherie . . . I am skilled in avoiding him. I'll meet you . . . so, where shall I meet you?'

She named a wine bar near to Covent Garden. There were plenty of eating places around there and it should be easy enough for him to find. She left him outside his apartment block and drove back her own flat, almost floating as she parked the car and went inside to get ready. There were several messages on her answering machine at home.

'I assume you struck gold as you didn't come back into the office and your mobile was switched off. I shall look forward to your piece.

Tomorrow morning please. I want it in this week's edition. Strike while the public's interested. And make it very personal, as we expect for our magazine. I know I can rely on you. Ciao.' Penelope's voice always sounded strident and impatient on the phone.

What a dilemma she faced. She was very attracted to this handsome French guy—half-French guy. He was so good looking. His eyes were the blackest brown she had ever seen with lashes that curled to a ridiculous length. His jet black hair, slightly too long, perhaps, made her want to run her fingers through it. She shook herself slightly. If she didn't write a piece for her Editor, she would be in trouble. If she did write it, Sacha would never want to see her again. Even if she told him the truth and didn't write anything, he might never want to see her again. Why was she suddenly so conscience stricken? She had chatted up many of the lesser celebrities and always got her story. Why was this one any different? Maybe she should make something up about someone but that was way too dangerous.

Amanda dressed carefully. She chose a slightly low cut, slinky crimson dress that showed off her curves and slim hips to perfection and then in a fit of discretion, changed it for a less blatant outfit. The crimson was much too obvious. She sensed that Sacha would go for a more groomed look. French women were always well-groomed,

7

weren't they? She picked out a more tailored, linen dress in a pale blue that exactly matched her eyes. She brushed her blonde hair and coiled it into a chignon, clasping it with her favourite silver clip. French made, she remembered. She applied minimal make up, again sensing that her date would prefer a natural look. She gave a twirl and nodded to herself. She'd do. She phoned for a cab and was ready. She still had made no decision about confessing the truth about herself but who cared? She intended to have a fun evening and face the consequences when she saw how things were progressing.

She arrived at the wine bar first and ordered a glass of house red. There were tables on the pavement outside but she chose to sit at a table near the window, so she could see Sacha arriving. She sipped her wine slowly, looking at each taxi as it stopped. When he was half an hour late, she began to feel anxious. Maybe he hadn't managed to shake off his guard after all. Maybe he had discovered who she really was. Maybe he had simply changed his mind. Maybe . . . maybe. Well, if he didn't show when she had finished her wine, she would leave. All the same, she sipped the wine so slowly that it could well have lasted her for most of the evening.

'Cherie? I'm so sorry to keep you waiting. I had a big argument with Fredo. I needed to sort it out before I left him.'

'I thought you'd changed your mind about coming,' she said weakly.

'Oh, no, ma cherie . . . how could you think that? I was looking forward to this evening so much.' The dark eyes looked rather as if they were pouring warm chocolate all over her. What a thought.

'I was looking out for you but I didn't see you arrive.'

'I came through a side door. I'm becoming paranoid about this wretched publicity. I can't stand all these so-called celebrity interest magazines. Makes anyone seem like something unusual when all the time, we are just people earning our living. Sensational gutter press. I hate it all.' Amanda wriggled uncomfortably. Should she just come out with the truth and call it a day? 'I'm sorry. You're looking wonderful. Sensational in fact. So refreshing to see a beautiful woman who doesn't try to force her sexuality on every man she meets.' She sent up a little prayer of gratitude that she hadn't worn the sexy red dress. 'Seems every girl I meet has the same message. But, I guess that goes with the territory. I can't tell you how nice it is to have an accidental meeting with someone who doesn't have an agenda. So, now I want to know all there is to know about you. Your life. Your family.'

Amanda was grateful that the low lighting in the wine bar hid her blushes, at least to some

9

extent. It was getting worse and worse with everything he said. Accidental meeting? It had been totally contrived and she certainly did have an agenda. If she really was one of the more unscrupulous journalists, she would wheedle out all sorts of things to use in her article but she wasn't. There were times when she actually hated the necessities of her work. What was more she really liked this man. Who wouldn't? A truly tall, dark and handsome cliché sitting so close to her so that his knee actually brushed her own, sending pulses of . . . well . . . whatever it was, it was more than pleasant. She was even fantasising about how it would feel to be held close by him.

'Amanda? Where were you? Am I boring you so much?'

'I'm sorry. I was . . . well, enjoying looking at you. Sorry, that sounds so corny. But you are a most attractive man. Gosh, should I be saying that? But I think there are several women around here who are incredibly jealous of me and my date.' She had already noticed the envious looks she was getting and felt very glad to be her.

'I am the lucky one. Perhaps it is I who is the object of such envy. So, ma belle Amanda, where are we going to eat?'

Feeling as if she were floating on air, she suggested a small bistro a couple of blocks away. It was a balmy summer evening and strolling along the busy cosmopolitan streets held its own special magic. There were people of all nationalities and delicious smells came from the many varied restaurants they passed.

'I'm starving,' she murmured. 'Despite that chocolate muffin I ate.'

'Me too.' He slipped his arm around her waist, a gesture that was comfortingly possessive. He felt her stiffen slightly and withdrew his arm. 'I am sorry. Perhaps I'm being too intimate on our first date.'

'No, no. It's fine. I like it.' Like it? Understatement of the century. It felt wonderful. She looped her own arm around his waist and smiled up at him. She felt dainty and feminine alongside this giant of a man. She could feel his powerful muscles, doubtless the product of many years spent practising. He may not be ranked anywhere in the world of tennis at this time but he was certainly climbing high in her own personal rankings.

'So, Amanda, cherie . . . tell me a little about yourself. What do you do?'

'Do? Erm . . .' She blabbered, stuck for words. What could she tell him? 'I er . . . sell magazines and such.'

'Really?' He sounded surprised. 'I'd have thought you'd have much more of a career than that.'

'It is a career,' she protested. If it wasn't for people who sold the magazines she wouldn't have a job at all.

'I'm sorry. I didn't mean to offend you. I'm

11

sure it's interesting to meet new people all the time. And I guess you have the chance to read the magazines. You'll understand my hatred of this sensational publicity. If they can't get a story, they just make something up.'

'You really do have a complex about this don't you?'

He shrugged. 'You know, if anyone believed everything that's been written about me, they'd think I have wife in every country and children by the dozen.'

'And you haven't of course?'

'How could you ask? I'm never in one place long enough even to begin a relationship let alone take it as far as marriage. No, I reckon I shall be a bachelor until I give up playing tennis.'

'But surely, most of the players get married? They always appear on television with the suitably glamorous wife sitting in the special box. The infant child wheeled in at an appropriate moment.'

'Maybe. But it's a difficult life and when I settle, I want it to be just that. At the moment I am travelling all the time. Eventually, I shall find someone and maybe have a kid or two. But I'm nowhere near that point in my life.'

Amanda smiled to hide a slight sense of disappointment. Then she grinned broadly. What on earth was she thinking of? She was having the evening of her life with a gorgeous man. Even if it was to be only the one. She

12

knew she was the envy of every other woman in the place. Sacha Manon. Rising tennis star. Once he'd left the country again she might be able to write a really sensational piece for *Personal*. One that would get Penelope Withenshaw jumping with excitement. After all, they were never likely to meet again, were they? He was speaking again.

'Somehow, you keep turning the subject round to me. I want to know all about you, please. Your home, family, what you want from life.'

What questions. Where did she start?

CHAPTER TWO

The evening passed in a sort of dream. Sacha was the perfect companion. Charming, complimentary, enthusiastic. Amanda was beginning to see why the gossip columns were so anxious to know all about him. He was totally charismatic but with a warmth and friendliness that was most unusual in her experience of minor celebrities.

'Amanda, ma chère Amanda, I have enjoyed our evening so very much. Will you accompany me for dinner again tomorrow? Then I have to leave. I am flying to America the following day to compete in another tournament. I have to practise during the day but I can be free by say, six-thirty?'

'I'd love to,' she whispered, almost breathless at the thought of seeing him again and delighted that he wanted to spend more time with her. Her conscience had been pushed well to the back and she already planned to deny that she had even got close to her assignment. Perhaps there would soon be another player she could catch up with, to write her piece.

'That's great. Shall I see you home?'

'Well, I came by cab so I'll have to call another. I think you are staying in the opposite direction so it isn't practical for you to see me home. Where do you want to meet tomorrow?'

'I'd like to see something of this city of yours, besides the odd restaurant and tennis courts. What do you suggest?'

'Well, depends what sort of thing do you want to see?'

'I've never been on this London Eye. How about we begin there?'

'Okay, you're on. Maybe we could take a river boat or have dinner somewhere near there?'

'Wonderful.' They ordered two cabs and stood waiting, He pulled her into his wonderfully strong arms and kissed her gently on the lips. 'Ma chère, my dear one. I have so enjoyed meeting you and I look forward with great pleasure to tomorrow. I'll meet you near the ticket office at the London Eye tomorrow.

14

Six thirty. Don't be late.'

She nodded, scarcely able to breathe.

She waved as her taxi drove away and blew him a kiss. But reality began to set in as she was driven back to her flat. What on earth was she doing fantasising about this man? He was a famous, or nearly famous sportsman. She was definitely not sporty. She quite enjoyed watching a bit of Wimbledon but that was the extent of her involvement since she had left school. Worst of all, she was exactly the sort of person he claimed to despise—a journalist looking for personal details. Besides, he was in England for literally a few weeks a year and had the choice of dozens—hundreds possibly—of gorgeous women. How could she ever be anything more than a companion with whom he might share the occasional meal? He'd called her something in French which had sounded totally intimate and meaningful and here she was, believing he had a serious, hidden message for her. Even the sexy way he pronounced her name made her feel very special. What rubbish! She could enjoy his company for one more evening and that was it. Nothing more. Tomorrow she needed to find her excuses for Penelope and look for another subject. There was no way she could write about this star, even if she never saw him again.

She spent a restless night, smiling at the memory of his final goodnight kiss. She'd had plenty of boyfriends in her time and plenty of kisses in her life but this one had seemed somehow special. She'd kissed several of her interview subjects, famous people in the public's gaze. They were so used to kissing everyone, it meant nothing. But none of them made her feel quite like Sacha had done. She had felt so safe in his arms and adored the feeling of strength that seemed to flow from him.

She rose early and planned her day. She needed to take a change of clothes into the office and, somehow, she must appear normal and casual in case someone suspected who she was really going out with that evening. If anyone got wind of it, she would be doomed. She would have to confess to Sacha who she really was. Write one of the scandalous pieces so loved by her boss and the public and hated by Sacha.

*   *   *

As Sacha tossed and turned for most of the night in his own apartment, rented for his stay in London, he wondered about his companion. She was so perfect. An English rose. Sweet and innocent compared to the women he usually met on the tour circuit. He knew nothing about her but he desperately wanted to know all there was to know. Her kiss was so fresh and he wanted more. Much more. What chance would he have? After tomorrow he would be away for several weeks. Someone like her couldn't be expected to wait till his next visit. Then his coach would be so demanding all the time. Practice, practice, practice. Damn it, he lived and breathed tennis but surely he was entitled to something more? But it was not in his master game plan. No serious relationships until he had at least tried to achieve his ambition.

Maybe he should follow his father's wishes and begin to play for Britain instead of France, if he was allowed. At least it would mean he could be in England more often. He might have more of a chance with this girl who had got to him like no one else ever had. Her slender body and that hair. Long, silky, blonde hair. He felt his mouth tighten, just like when he was playing and felt that surge of determination he needed to win. It was tempting to move to this country permanently. In Britain, he would also have a higher profile in the tennis world. Maybe he should give up tennis altogether and return to France and help run the family vineyard. He shook himself. This was all so foolish. He had picked up some woman outside the tennis courts, one of a dozen who stood around and here he was, already fantasising about some sort of future with her. She could be married for all he knew. But something told him she wasn't. No sign of a wedding ring. She wasn't the type to cheat on anyone. Those wonderful clear blue eyes were so totally honest. And her hair. He came back to the thought. He loved blondes and suspected Amanda's was long, smooth and straight when it was let loose. It would be heaven to stroke it, to caress it when it was spread over his pillow. He rose from his rumpled bed and took a shower. Just over 12 hours and he would see her again. He could hardly wait.

*   *   *

Penelope called Amanda into her office first thing.

'So, how did you do with the tennis people? Manage to nab anyone?'

'I'm sorry. I tried but they were all rushed out by their coaches or guarded by their not so tame Rottweilers. I'll give it another try tomorrow. I have to finish the piece on celebrity maternity fashions today.'

'Don't leave it too late. It will be the major Wimbledon fortnight before long and everyone will be plastering their issues with tennis gossip. I want us in there first. One of these sexy looking, rising stars, preferably. Someone the tabloids haven't reached yet.'

'Okay. Leave it with me.' Penelope had described Sacha to perfection.

'Don't let me down. You look tired. Get an early night.'

'Sure.'

'Unless it's one of those tennis guys. In that case, you should stay on as late as it takes.' Penelope laughed.

Amanda blushed, hoping her boss hadn't noticed. She'd be furious if she realised the real situation. She left the office and went back to her desk. The other girls looked at her curiously.

'So what's the news?' Jenny, her best friend asked.

'Nothing much.'

'You don't bring a silk shirt, smart linen trousers and your best strappy sandals into the office unless you have a date. So, come on. Who is he? Where did you meet him and how long have you known him?'

'Shut up, Jen. Yes. I have got a date but it's only casual. Just someone I met and in any case, he's going away tomorrow so there's nothing more to it than a pleasant evening ahead. Okay?'

'Did you have any luck with the tennis interview?' she asked suddenly. Amanda coloured again. She could keep nothing from Jenny but could she really trust her to keep this particular secret?

'They were all guarded like the Crown Jewels,' she said quickly. 'You wouldn't believe the security.'

'I guess. Danger of kidnapping and everything. And those awful celeb magazines

19

who hang around, hoping to dish the dirt.'

'Too right. Never go near them myself.'

'It's a pretty lousy job we do, isn't it? I can't think why people want to know all this so-called intimate stuff about anyone really.'

'Part of the fantasy I s'pose. "What I would do if I was rich", sort of thing. Well, someone will doubtless be delighted to know what Jemima Super Star plans to wear for the last two months of her pregnancy. If I ever get round to writing it up. Speak to you later.'

'You can bet you will. I haven't given up on hearing about your mystery man. I need all the details. Height. weight. Inside leg measurement.'

'Get lost, Jen.' She turned on her computer and picked up her notebook. She struggled to concentrate, wondering what Sacha was doing at this moment. Had he given her any thought at all? She doubted it as he would be busily packing ready for his next trip and he'd mentioned something about practising. Even when he wasn't actually playing in a tournament, he needed to keep playing. Keep training to hone that amazing body.

She shook herself back to reality. She began to jot down a few notes. Just for her own interest and if she did indeed write up a piece, it would ensure she didn't forget details. It was a dangerous thing to do. Anyone could peek over her shoulder and get the wrong impression. Quickly, she tore off the sheet of

20

paper and screwed it up. She stuffed it into her handbag, intending to put it through the office shredder.

*   *   *

The day dragged on until at last it was five o'clock and she could think about leaving. She tidied her desk, shut down the computer and went to the rest room to change. Inevitably, Jenny was lying in wait.

'So, come on. Details please.'

'You sound worse than our esteemed boss lady.'

'Oh, ha, ha. There must be a juicy story behind your date or you wouldn't be so coy about telling me. Spill the beans.'

'I told you. Just someone I met casually. A visitor to these shores and he wanted to go on the Eye. I said I'd go with him. End of story.'

'That's only the opening line,' Jenny persisted. 'Where did you meet him? What's he like?'

'I met him while I was waiting for a train and we got talking. He's not really my type at all. Too quiet and he probably doesn't even dance. I'm doing my bit for international relations. Now, if you don't mind, I need to change.'

'Okay. But I'm still not satisfied. Didn't you have your car yesterday? So what were doing on a train?'

'Ever thought of signing on with MI5?'

'Never. I'm just an investigative journalist who's very good at her job and first class at spotting evasion. I shall get to the truth, young lady. Persistence is my middle name.'

'And I never said I'd met him yesterday, when I certainly did have my car, Miss Clever Clogs.'

Amanda sighed and locked herself into a cubicle, hoping Jenny would get bored and disappear. It was already getting late and she still had to cross London in the rush hour. She changed her clothes and stuffed the worn ones into a plastic carrier. She would leave it here till tomorrow and take it home after work.

'Still here, I see,' she muttered angrily to her friend, as she freshened her make-up in front of the long mirror.

'My, my. The full works. Have I seen that outfit before?' asked her friend.

'No. Got it in the sale last week.'

'Good colour,' Jenny said as she felt the quality of the royal blue silk shirt. 'Nice feel. Mmm, he should like that. Okay, I give up— enjoy.' She left the room but opened the door again and called in, 'But I'll want all the info tomorrow. And I mean all. Bye.'

'Thank heavens for small mercies,' Amanda muttered and she clasped a gold chain round her neck. She dashed outside and hailed a taxi. She was definitely going to be late. She hoped that her tennis player was suffering the same fate. The traffic was horrendous. At six-twenty she was still a mile away. She wished she'd thought to exchange phone numbers. She stared helplessly at her mobile, knowing it was useless. An image of the tall athlete flashed into her mind. Was he really as gorgeous as she remembered? His eyes couldn't really be almost black and his hair didn't really curl quite as she remembered. Would she actually recognise him? She only had a broad image of him, if the truth be told.

At last the taxi pulled up and she paid the driver. She stood looking round at the crowds of people. Where was he? Maybe she dreamt it all. Hesitantly, she stepped away from the pavement towards the crowds thronging around the ticket booths, gazing around for her date. Surely he hadn't given up on her? She was only minutes late and he would realise how bad the traffic was. Maybe he'd thought better of it and decided against turning up himself. Or maybe he was simply late, as she was.

'Hello, ma'am. Do you think I could interest you in a ride on the Eye, followed by dinner?'

'Oh, Sacha, you came.'

'You didn't doubt me, did you?' He was just as gorgeous as she remembered, in fact even more so. He was wearing beautifully cut light grey trousers and silk shirt almost the same shade, perhaps just a little lighter. His broad shoulders and slim waist were shown off to advantage. He had a light blue sweater, probably cashmere, she thought, slung over his shoulder in case it was cooler later. 'You look lovely,' he remarked as he kissed her on both cheeks. She felt the heat rising.

'You look good yourself. Sorry I was late. The traffic was awful. Were you waiting for long?'

'A while. I was impatient to see you and arrived far too early. But I have already bought the tickets to save us from queuing.' He held out his hand and drew her towards him. She felt the earth topple slightly as they touched. She hoped she would never get quite used to the phenomenon . . . it was a powerful effect and almost addictive. Her lips remembered his good night kiss from yesterday and tingled in anticipation of renewing the sensation. 'You are even more beautiful than I remembered.'

She gave an involuntary shiver of anticipation. 'Let's go then. I haven't been here since it first opened.' She felt sure her voice shook slightly.

Hand in hand they walked along the paths and stood to wait in line with the other ticket holders. They chatted easily, catching up on their day. Already, they seemed to have an ease in their relationship that often took weeks to achieve. She managed to avoid too many direct questions about her own work, showing great interest in the way he had spent his time since last night. Four gruelling hours on the practice courts, followed by a swim and some time spent in the gym.

'Wow. I'm exhausted just thinking of it. No wonder you're so fit.'

'It's all routine. But, I admit I am a little tired today. I didn't sleep well.'

'I'm sorry. I expect it was the anti-climax after losing yesterday. You must be very disappointed.'

'Not at all. I was thinking of a beautiful English rose who has filled my senses completely. I wished I had your cell phone number so I could have called you. To make sure you weren't just a dream.' She felt the heat rising to her cheeks. Did he mean it? He had really been thinking of her last night?

'I thought of you too.' Her voice was shaking slightly.

'So, was it a busy day at the shop?'

'Shop?' she said puzzled. Then she remembered her fib. 'Oh, the shop. Yes, quite busy.'

'Here we go. This is us, next gondola.' They stepped inside and took a position near the edge. 'Oh, I expected it would move more quickly,' Sacha commented as they moved upwards. 'It's so slow you are hardly aware of the movement at all. It's a lovely city, isn't it? The buildings remind me of Paris in many ways. Huge structures with many windows, clustering along the side of a river.' As they

25

rose and the view expanded, he was silent. He slipped an arm round her shoulder and she nestled against him, loving the feel of his firm body. His arm was sending pulses of heat through her, suggesting that her entire body was ready to join in with the conspiracy. Once more, she was aware of how tall he was. She was no dwarf at five foot nine but still he seemed to tower over her.

'How tall are you?' she asked.

'Six foot, four inches,' he said slowly. 'You still use feet and inches?'

'I certainly do. I think the kids today are used to metric.' She laughed. 'Here I am, looking down on London with a gorgeous man and comparing the metric system with imperial.'

'But it's important. The differences. Vive la différence.' They watched as London passed them by and all too soon, the ride ended. 'That was excellent. Thank you for sharing it with me.' She smiled back at him. 'Now, where are we going to eat? Shall we walk along the riverside and see what we can find?'

They strolled along the South Bank, passing theatre goers and those like themselves who were enjoying another fine summer evening. Amanda felt a mixture of emotions. Joy at being with him, sadness that he was leaving the next day. Longing for this new relationship to continue. They headed into the town and found a small restaurant where they had dinner. As the meal came to an end, they became silent, their fingers touching across the table.

'I can't bear to leave you ma belle. But I am committed to this trip.'

'I know. It's much too soon for us to be parted. We hardly know each other but I feel we have known each for ever. I shall miss you.'

'And I, you. Will you give me your cell number?'

'Mobile number,' she corrected. 'Of course.' She took out her diary and wrote it on a page and tore it out. 'Can I have yours?' She punched the numbers into her own phone and smiled at him. 'Will you text?'

'Of course. We can keep in touch. Hey, you dropped something.' He leaned down and picked up the crumpled sheet of paper on which she had made notes about him and then forgotten to shred. She went pale as she realised what it was.

'Sorry. Just rubbish. Give it to me please.'

'But rubbish in a lady's purse is utterly fascinating,' he teased, starting to unwrap it.

'Please, Sacha. It's private.'

'Okay. But you have me interested now. What is it that you so much want to hide? A secret note from a lover? A billet doux?'

'Of course not. I don't have any lovers, secret or otherwise.'

'Then don't be afraid. I'm sorry, I shouldn't tease. But it is clearly something you don't want me to see. Here. Keep your secret.' He tossed it back and she grabbed it and pushed it deep inside her bag. 'I was wondering,' he said huskily, 'if you might consider coming to the States to see me? I have to be there for three weeks. You could come over for a week or so. If your shop can spare you of course.' Her heart leapt at the excitement of his suggestion, but reality hit her.

'Oh, Sacha. I don't know. It's a bit sudden isn't it? You hardly know me.'

'Maybe. But I'd like to change that. I shall need to see you before three whole weeks are through. I have a series of small tournaments and matches to play. I won't be back in England for possibly four weeks I guess.'

He lived in a different world, she was thinking. She couldn't drop everything and dash off to America just like that. A week's holiday from her job took a great deal of organising.

'I can't take holiday just like that.'

'Give your notice. You'll find another job easily. I will pay for your flight and accommodation. I will probably take an apartment as usual. Fredo is certain to have something organised.'

Amanda's mind was in total melt down. If she handed in her notice, it would mean the end of her career and she certainly wasn't ready for that. She hardly knew the man, however much she wanted to change that state of affairs. Besides, she certainly couldn't accept his paying for her visit. Maybe he wasn't quite as nice as she thought. What did he expect of her? Was she to be just another hanger on? A groupie?

'Sacha . . . I'm very flattered by your suggestion but I simply can't do it.'

'I'll show you New York. Though I will be playing some of the time, I can still have plenty of opportunity to take you to places. I will be proud to show you off to my friends and colleagues. But maybe, you are not so pleased with me. You do not feel as I do?'

'You're moving too fast. Only yesterday you were saying you have no plans to settle down.'

'I'm not inviting you to settle clown, as you put it. I simply want to be with you. For us to spend time together. Is that so wrong of me? I enjoy your company. Isn't that what you said to me last night?'

'I guess. But I'm simply not able to reorganise my life just to take a holiday. I have to book it in advance. Arrange cover for my . . . for my work.' She'd so nearly said column. She was feeling guilty. Dreadfully guilty that he thought she was something she wasn't.

They'd come a long way this evening. She was beginning to know the real man. He had lived in the rolling hills of Provence for much of his life and was used to helping out in the family vineyard. He was knowledgeable about wines and seemed to have a loving family. Her

29

feelings of guilt about her own work had made her reticent to talk about herself but he had seemed content with what she had said.

'If you are certain. I'll call you tomorrow, before I fly out. It's acceptable to use your cell phone? Your bosses won't be angry that I call you at work?'

'No. That's fine. Call me when you like. No problem.'

'So, for now it's goodnight, Amanda,' he said sadly, 'But I sincerely hope that I will see you again very soon.'

'Thank you for a lovely evening.' Amanda felt remarkably close to tears as he drew her close. They kissed gently but there was tension growing between them. A group of young men passed them and called out lewd comments. She felt Sacha stiffen and he drew in his breath. 'It's all right,' she whispered. 'Ignore them.'

'Perhaps they are jealous of my good fortune.'

'I should go now, before it becomes even more impossible to leave you.'

'Then don't go.'

'I must. Call me. I also hope we'll see other again soon.' Blocking the threatening tears, she turned away and hailed a cab She left him standing on the pavement, his hand raised in a gesture of farewell. She sniffed into a hankie and wiped her eyes.

CHAPTER THREE

Inevitably, sleep was almost impossible. Her body was one hundred percent in favour of catching the next flight to America. Her brain was behaving more sensibly and was only ninety percent committed to the idea. If Penelope guessed the real reason for a sudden trip, she'd probably offer to pay first class fares. The chance of getting in on the tennis circuit first hand, well, it would open no end of doors and provide the dirt for a whole series of articles.

Suddenly, she felt her own sense of guilt about her job when seen from her victims' point of view. It was somewhat sleazy and unpleasant. She knew already that she cared rather too much about Sacha; she couldn't hurt him in any way. But then, Penelope didn't have any deep feelings to intrude on her professionalism. She must have some sort of life outside work but if so, she never let it show and seemed to find it strange that anyone else did. How could Amanda possibly organise a week off without letting the real truth slip? With Jenny on her case, it would be nigh on impossible.

When she did doze off to sleep, her dreams were filled with fantasies that actually made her blush when she woke up and remembered them. What was this man doing to her? How could someone like him, be interested in her? She was an ordinary working girl like so many thousands of others. He had clearly said that serious relationships were not in his current game plan. Why should she be so scared? Wasn't she a twenty-first century woman, well able to look after herself? She was a tough journalist, wasn't she? Capable, professional . . . but dared she go to America to join him? Perhaps she should ask if she could have time off? Then, when her request was turned down, she'd at least have a proper excuse. She should not get too involved. No man could be this perfect. He must have some darker side that she hadn't yet discovered.

'Could I have a word?' she asked Penelope the next morning.

'Only if it's to ask how many words I need for the tennis star article.'

'Em . . . no. Sorry. Nothing doing on that front yet. I was actually wondering if I could book a week's leave?' Penelope looked back at the sheaf of papers on her desk.

'You know where the rota is. Just book it.'

'Well, actually, I wondered about next week.'

'Four weeks' notice. You know the rules. Unless it's an emergency.'

'Not exactly.'

'Not sick are you?'

'No. Okay. Just thought it worth asking.'

32

Penelope appeared even more engrossed. 'Okay then. Er, thanks.' That was that. She didn't want to go anyway, did she? Her mobile rang. She tucked herself behind the water dispenser and tried to speak quietly.

'Sacha? Hi.'

'Hello. I'm just on my way to the airport. Thought I'd say good morning.'

'Nice to hear you.'

'Did you think any more about coming over to visit with me?'

'I asked my boss but she said no.'

'That's ridiculous. Everyone can take a holiday.'

'We have to give notice. So there's someone to cover for us.'

'For heaven's sake. Why don't you finish with the ridiculous job? You can surely get another one easily enough. I can't wait for nearly a whole month to see you again.'

'I like my job. It isn't always as easy as you think to get another.'

'A job in a magazine shop? Don't be so ridiculous. I guess you simply don't want to come over. Maybe I'm mistaking the messages you were sending to me.'

'No, Sacha. You're not.' Maybe this was the moment to come clean and tell him the truth. Oh, yes, that would be a very clever move. That would be goodbye forever and not even a 'nice knowing you' footnote to soften the blow. All the same, her work was hardly in a

33

magazine shop. Her silly, miscalculated lie was coming home to roost. 'I'm sorry. It's all too hurried. It's not the way we work here,' she mumbled. Jenny came over to get some water. 'Look, I'm sorry. I have to go now. I'll call you later.'

'Maybe I will be able to answer. But I'll be on the plane before long. Au revoir.' And he was gone.

'Did I interrupt something?' Jenny asked with poorly faked innocence.

'Not really. I was about done.' She gave a sigh and felt a sense of depression clouding over her. She'd handled that call so badly. On the other hand, Sacha wasn't exactly being very understanding. This had been their first phone call on parting and she'd blown it. Maybe having him call her at the office wasn't such a good idea.

'There's clearly something going on. How was the mysterious date?'

'Good. He's gone away now so I'm just feeling a bit down. It did look as if it might go somewhere but hey, that's life. On to the next assignment.'

'So, he was an assignment, was he?' Jenny persisted.

'Of course not. He was just a guy I met and now he's gone. Okay? So, what are you working on?'

They returned to office chat and safer ground. The morning crawled by. Whatever

Amanda did, Sacha's face with his halo of raven black hair seemed to float in front of her eyes. Concentration was impossible.

'For goodness' sake, Amanda. Where are you today?'

'Sorry? What?' she snapped.

'I asked you for the third time, are we going to get some lunch?'

'Sorry. I think I'll work through.' It might even give her the opportunity to call Sacha again and try to explain. Explain what, she wondered. She glanced at her watch. He'd be on the plane by now so he wouldn't be able to answer. 'Oh, hang it. I'll come with you . . . as long as you drop the Spanish Inquisition routine.'

'I don't know what you mean,' Jenny replied indignantly. She had no intention of letting anything drop. There was a juicy story lying under Amanda's evasiveness and she had every intention of finding out every last bit of gossip.

*　　　*　　　*

Sacha sat in his cab en route for the airport. After the call to Amanda, he stuffed his phone into his pocket and stared through the window.

'What's up?' demanded Fredo, his coach and companion. They were speaking in French as Fredo's English wasn't brilliant.

'Nothing. I was hoping for a better

35

response.'

'And is this something to do with your mysterious absence from the apartment the last couple of evenings?'

'Well, yes.'

'Hey come on. You know the rules. No women during the season.'

'But according to you, the tournament season seems to last the entire year. No sooner do we finish one round in the Northern Hemisphere than you're starting to book me up in the Southern.'

'If you want to get anywhere, it has to happen soon. You're getting older. Time slips away. Okay, for you, maybe it is already too late for the really big tournaments. Perhaps the grand slams are beyond you but you make a more than decent living from the rest. There's plenty of time for women and everything else in a few years' time.'

Sacha sighed and closed his eyes. Two days ago, he would have agreed. Before Amanda. She was his dream, his perfect woman. What was it about her? They had kissed a few times and spent time together over a couple of meals but his tennis ambitions had been knocked right back. After all the years of training and practice, how could he simply drop out of it now? And all for a woman he scarcely knew.

'You scare me Sacha. I've invested a lot of time and effort into you. I can't believe you plan to give up just like that. You're crazy.'

'I think I may be in love.'

'Get her out of your system somehow. Can't be that difficult. A guy with your looks should have no problem.'

'It's not just any woman that will do, thanks all the same. I'm trying to persuade her to come out and join me. I could do with a few diversions.'

Fredo looked thoughtful. If his rising star was serious about this girl, whoever she was, maybe he needed to do some investigating of his own. He wasn't having some female messing around with Sacha's head. He needed his man clear, sharp and focussed. He had three, maybe four more years to get anywhere near the top before his time was through. This year he'd broken into the top 90 players in the world rankings and that was quite some achievement for a man of his age. Teenagers seemed to rule these days.

'Okay. So who is she, what does she do? Do you want me to organise something? A diversion?'

'Of course not. She's a girl I met outside the courts one day. We made a connection. She's not some groupie looking for reflected glory. She's open and honest and with no hidden agendas. Needless to say, she's also gorgeous. Amazing blonde hair. A real English rose. Gorgeous figure and perfect dress sense.'

'Oh, worse than I thought.' Fredo groaned. 'Much worse. Just settle for one of the girls who hang around the circuit. Don't complicate matters.'

'Don't worry. I'm not giving up. I'll train as hard as you wish but it doesn't stop me wanting Amanda. I'll keep trying to persuade her to come and join us in America. She works in a shop so it shouldn't be too difficult.'

'A shop girl? Great. This gets better and better. Not even a refugee from an Aussie soap? No nubile little French girl? Any of these would enhance his reputation, but oh, no, he picks a shop girl.'

'It's an honest job.' Why did he feel he needed to be so defensive? 'Look, mind your own business, hey? I'm going to have some control over my own life from now on. You're not my parent, even if you behave like one. I work hard and don't forget I keep you employed, might I add.'

Fredo closed his eyes and feigned bored sleep. His mind was racing however. This latest affair sounded much more serious than any of his other casual encounters. His player was certainly charismatic enough and his avoidance of publicity added that extra intriguing quality. Maybe it was time to up his profile a little and release just a hint of gossip in the right quarters. He'd have to be careful though. One hint of where the gossip came from and he'd be out of a job. However good he was.

                    *   *   *

As she sat alone in her flat, Amanda reflected that it was less than 24 hours since she had said goodbye to Sacha. Already it seemed a world away and she was forgetting what he looked like. She switched on her laptop and typed his name into a search engine. There he was. Why hadn't she thought of this before? There were pictures and details of his career. Though he had won a few tournaments, his profile was far less significant in Britain than many of the major players. She searched further, looking for any items of gossip she could find. It was thin on the ground. That figured. Went with all his statements about being shy of publicity. She printed off one of the pictures and slightly foolishly, she thought, pinned it over her computer. She picked up her mobile and wrote a text. Innocent and casual, she hoped.

Hope journey was good. Best of luck with tour. Show 'em who's top. Should she sign it *love*? Everyone did. It meant little or nothing. All the same, she merely signed it 'A'. She pressed send before she could change her mind. Then she stared at her phone for the next ten minutes, willing it to ring. Nothing. Why, oh why, hadn't she agreed to go and visit this wonderful man in America? Just think what her friends would have said. What did they matter? Why should she even contemplate trying to impress any of them? She went to bed. If Sacha replied to her text, it would be waiting next day.

* * *

It seemed an interminable few days. Texts and a few fairly brief chats did nothing to enhance her previous feeling of connection with the tennis player. She found herself scouring sports pages for any mention of the man. She even hoped he was losing his matches so that he would return sooner. If only she'd had the courage, she could have been out there with him enjoying the whole experience.

'You've become a total recluse,' Jenny complained. 'We're going to that new club tonight and I simply won't take no for an answer. You're coming too and you're going to enjoy a good night.'

'Oh, I don't think so. I'm not in the mood.'

'Well, tough. It's partly for work. We're supposed to seek out the rich and famous at one of the hottest new nightspots. Penelope has suggested a joint piece from us and wants something by tomorrow afternoon. She's not best pleased with you, young woman after your failure to secure a tennis story. Says you're going off lately. So, you see, I'm solely responsible for salvaging your career.'

Amanda sighed and nodded and they arranged to meet outside the club at ten-thirty.

'I think I'm getting too old for all these late nights.'

'See? Like I said. Fun's gone out of your life. You're not in love or anything stupid are you?'

'Of course not,' she lied. Love must be the only explanation for the way she was feeling. If it hadn't been extremely dangerous, she would have liked to carry a picture of Sacha with her at all times but he would be too easily recognised and that could lead to too many questions.

She did her best to join in with the others at the nightclub. She spotted one or two people who might fit in with the article they were supposed to write. She even went over to a young footballer and his latest girlfriend and asked if she might take a photo of them. He had been in the newspapers lately following a signing to a major club. Amanda knew that he was single and that she would not be starting some scandal by her picture.

'Oh, go on, love,' urged the young girl. 'I'd like to be seen in a mag with you. The others would be dead jealous.' She draped herself over her escort who looked suitably relaxed about the relationship and Amanda took several shots with the digital camera. For these casual trips, digital cameras were quite adequate, as spontaneous photographs were much better than contrived photo shoots with the professional photographers hanging around.

'Good little cameras those,' the footballer muttered. 'At least you had the decency to ask first. Thanks.'

'And your companion's name? Just for the record,' she asked.

'Tell 'er then love,' he suggested, as if he didn't know.

'Er, Chanterelle.'

'I see. Thanks.' She refrained from asking why the girl, or her parents, had picked the name of a type of mushroom. Evidently, it sounded reasonably glamorous to her ears. Amanda made a note of the names and moved away with a smile. The evening wore on and finally, she suggested to Jenny that they probably had enough material for a short article.

'You are truly no fun any more, Amanda Jayne Derry. Have you had a personality transplant? Either that or I go back to my theory—you're in love.'

'I'm not even sure what love is.'

'The sort of reaction you're currently displaying. Mind somewhere else, distracted, clearly thinking of someone else. Jump like mad when the phone rings . . . you get the picture.'

'So, maybe I am. Just don't have anyone close to be in love with. Now, if you don't mind, I'm going home.' She fought her way through the heaving mass of gyrating bodies and couldn't wait to get some fresh air. In love? Me, she thought. No chance.

Her mobile rang and she jumped. Who on earth could be calling at this time of night? Could it be . . .? The screen displayed International.

The night was warm and she drew to one side of the pavement, crowded with club goers even at this late hour.

'Hello?' she murmured, hoping it was him.

'Hello, Amanda. I was missing you.'

'It's the middle of the night,' she said weakly. Her knees were shaking. In fact, most of her was shaking.

'I'm sorry. Did I wake you? I don't think so. I can hear noises . . .'

'No. I was working. I'm just going home now.'

'What time is it?'

'One o'clock.'

'What sort of shop keeps you working till one o'clock? I am puzzled.' The way he said the word 'puzzled' was just so incredibly sexy. She smiled.

'I've been missing you too. Silly isn't it?'

'But still, you will not come to join me in America? Not even to see me?'

'Oh, Sacha. I can't. Truly I can't.'

'Then I simply have to come back to London to be with you.'

'Really?' The delight sounded in her voice. 'But how can you? I can't let you abandon

43

your career for me.'

'I've had to drop out of the next tournament. I pulled a muscle and need to rest before Wimbledon. I can work on it over there just as easily as here.'

'I'm sorry to hear that. But it's wonderful you can come back. I can't wait to see you again.'

'I'm pleased. Fredo is angry though.'

'When will you get here?'

'I hope to pick up a flight tomorrow.'

Jenny came out of the club with a couple of other girls.

'Oh, hello. You're still here,' she said. 'And on the phone again. I said you were in love. Hi, sexy,' she called out, putting her face near the phone.

'Go away,' hissed Amanda. 'This is private.' She turned away from her friend. 'Sorry. I'll have to go. Call me again soon.' She switched off the phone and laughed out loud. 'You know Jen, I think you might have something there, but love is an awfully big word. One of the biggest I've ever heard of. But you might be right.'

CHAPTER FOUR

Two seemingly endless days later, Sacha phoned. 'I'm just leaving the airport. Where shall we meet?' Amanda's heart practically stopped beating for a second or two. 'I've had to take a taxi as there is so much luggage. I'm booked into a hotel near to the Wimbledon area. That's the only place I know.'

'Okay. How about we meet at the wine bar where we first met? Then we can decide what to do. Presumably, you will want to eat?'

'Fine. Six-thirty suit you?'

'Perfect.' He rang off.

'Who's perfect?' the ever curious Jen asked. 'Oh, no, don't tell me. Mystery Man's returned.'

Unable to hide her smile, Amanda nodded. 'I'm seeing him later. Heavens, I've got nothing to wear. Emergency shopping at lunch time.'

'So where's he taking you?'

'Not sure. We'll decide when we meet. I just need something to change into. There won't be time to go home.'

'I can't come with you. I've got an interview with someone who's just finished with one of the members of some awful pop group who keep seeming to crop up everywhere. Finishing with one of them sounds about the most sensible thing she could have done. I'll pick up the requisite pack of tissues and brace myself to be sympathetic. "Oh, you poor thing. What plans do you have for the future?" You know the lines. Now, about this shopping. Do you want to go after work, if I'm back in time?'

45

'No worries. I can still just about manage to choose a dress myself.'

Her morning's work was finished in record time and she rushed down to the nearest stores to find something new for the evening ahead. He liked her in blue. In fact, he'd only seen her in blue on the two occasions they had met. It seemed impossible to think that it was only twice they had been out together. She felt as if she had known Sacha all her life. She picked out a simple trouser outfit in light green. A bargain in the sale and not blue this time. Her old bag and shoes would do. She didn't really want the expense of new shoes as well. She floated on her personal cloud back to the office and found an angry Penelope waiting for her.

'What's this rubbish you've left on my desk? You always used to be one of my best girls but this is flat, uninspiring and . . . well, it simply won't do. If you don't buck up, you'll be leaving us.'

'I'm sorry,' she mumbled. 'I'll check it through again and see if I can liven it up a bit.'

'You're slipping Amanda. Lost your sparkle. Maybe you needed to take that break you asked for. Get your copy ready for the next issue by tomorrow afternoon and then you can take the next week off. Try to pull yourself together.'

'Really?' she gasped. 'That would be fantastic.' Perfect in every way, her mind was saying. She could spend more time with Sacha and not have to worry about keeping her secret or pretend to Jenny that there was nothing significant happening each day. 'What about the usual four weeks' notice you said I needed?'

'I'm counting this as an emergency leave. Your concentration is all over the place. I can't do with you like this. I want you back the following week bright and shiny and full of new energy.'

'Thanks, Penelope. Thank you so much. And I really will try to make the piece better before I go this evening.' Her grin was uncontrollable.

The Editor walked away, wondering how being on the verge of dismissal could bring such delight to the girl. If she wasn't so good, Amanda would have gone right away but Penelope felt in her bones that she had great potential and would allow her this one chance. She assumed it was some sort of crisis with a man, silly girl. Her career needed to come first at all times. She should realise it rapidly and get to grips with it.

Desperately trying to concentrate on the rejected piece of work, Amanda added, deleted and generally tidied up the article. Baby fashions did little for her but flicking through a collection of press pictures, she was able to put something together based on sightings of celebrities and their offspring. *Talk about scraping the barrel*, she thought and crossing her fingers that dear Penelope would like it.

By five o'clock she could scarcely sit still and finally gave up and went into the cloakroom to change. Fortunately, Jenny hadn't returned so she was spared an interrogation. As they all spent a lot of time out of the office seeking stories, nobody checked on precise working hours so she was able to get away early and best of all, unnoticed by her colleagues.

Her knees were positively knocking by the time she arrived at the wine bar. She sat in the same window seat as before and ordered a mineral water. For the umpteenth time, she checked her hair and makeup in her little mirror. Suppose he didn't feel the same way when he saw her again? Then, maybe they wouldn't recognise each other. Then she caught a glimpse of him as he strode along the now crowded pavement. Her heart did a quick somersault. If anything, he was even more beautiful than she remembered. Could a man be beautiful? This one was, in her eyes at least.

'Amanda. My darling Amanda. You came.' He took her hands and almost lifted her off her chair. He wrapped her in his arms and kissed her. She forgot about being embarrassed as she revelled in seeing him again. He also had forgotten his paranoia about keeping himself out of the gossip columns. But luckily nobody noticed this

48

young couple greeting each other so happily.

'Sacha, it's so good to see you.' Breathless, she sat down again before her legs collapsed beneath her. He ordered wine for both of them and held her hand as they drank.

'I have missed you so very much. Fredo has not forgiven me for leaving and threatens to abandon me for ever.'

'But you can't be without him. Isn't this all a bit rash?'

'I don't care. He has gone back to France to work while I decided to come here. Besides, I have to nurse an injury. He's organised it all for me. Fortunately, it's my right shoulder and I am a left handed player. It affects my service of course, you know when I toss up the ball but it is not as bad as if it were my left arm. So, I have almost a week of freedom with just a small time commitment to have the physiotherapy each day.'

'Fantastic. Really good news from me too, I've just been given next week off. Evidently I'm not . . .' she paused. She needed to be careful what she said. 'I'm not working as well as I should be. In need of a holiday my boss told me. Needless to say, I didn't argue at all. Especially not when I knew you were going to be in London.'

'I have an idea,' Sacha said, a grin spreading across his face. He bit his bottom lip, looking thoughtful. 'No, I'll say nothing. Not yet. I'll say it later. It's a rather major idea actually. I just hope you will agree with me. Let's go and find some dinner now. I'm starving.' He emptied his glass and reached for her hand. 'Come, let's walk.'

'What is it? What did you want to say? You're just teasing me.'

'Later. I'll talk about it later.'

As they strolled through the evening crowds, he rested his arm on her shoulder. It felt good. She looked up at him and knew this was exactly where she most wanted to be. They ate dinner outside at one of the bistros, enjoying the warm evening. It was surprisingly warm for April.

'So, what was your idea?'

'I hope you will agree to it. Amanda, will you marry me? I have fallen in love with you and I know there will never be anyone else who can make me feel as you do.'

'Marry you? Marry you?' She gulped down the last of her wine, almost choking with the shock of his words. 'Do you really mean it?'

'Of course. I would never ask you something like this if I didn't mean it.'

'But we hardly know each other. We only met a few days ago. I mean, you know nothing about me. I'm just an ordinary girl, nothing special. You're a rising star. You'll always work hard to make your career a success.'

'There is more to my idea. If you do agree to marry me, we can get married right away. While I am staying here in London. You also have a holiday so it's all perfect. But we shall need to keep it a complete secret.'

'You're completely mad. But so am I. Yes, yes please. I'd love to marry you. And keeping it secret suits me very well. Oh Sacha, I love you too. So very much. Since we met, I have thought of you all of the time. You are always there, in my mind. This is why my work has become so poor. I can't seem to concentrate on anything. My best friend has been teasing me all the time, saying I must be in love. Now I understand why. When exactly do you want us to have this secret wedding?' He was looking puzzled.

'I don't really understand how selling magazines and papers can be damaged by your lack of attention.' He frowned and she blushed, knowing it was now or never to make her confession. But she dared not ruin the moment so it became never. 'Eh bien. Marriage? Now, of course. Right away. But my darling, can we get married so quickly? Is it possible? Are there not papers and things to be agreed?'

'I think you have to get a special licence. I don't know how quickly that can be done but I can find out.'

As she went into work the next day, she could barely speak to anyone. The excitement was filling her brain but still, she knew she must tell no one. It was one of the hardest things she'd ever had to do. She looked up information about licences on her computer and discovered to her disappointment that there had to be a proof of residence before a licence could be issued. She was all right and fulfilled all the requirements but from what she could make out, she thought Sacha had to stay in London for a week to qualify. She called Sacha and explained what they had to do. They arranged to meet at the registry office at lunchtime. It would be a week before they could have their licence. But this would be a week when they could be together and get to know each other a little more.

'I don't know how I shall wait,' he told her.

'I want us to wait. I always promised myself that I wasn't going to be like all the others. I want to wait until we are married before anything, well anything happens. We can explore London. Make our plans. We have the rest of our lives to be married so what is one more week? But now, I must go back to work and finish everything before I leave this evening.'

'And I have to go and see my physiotherapist. I'll see you this evening.'

Amanda was bubbling over with excitement for the entire afternoon. She worked as hard as she could with a brain that was trying desperately to make long term plans for her own life. Somehow, she had to complete one more article before she could leave. It was after five before she even lifted her head from her computer. Jenny had been staring at her most of the afternoon but had said nothing.

'Okay. You're going nowhere until you spill the beans. Something is going on in your tiny little mind and I intend to know what it is.' Her friend stared back at her, wondering how she could say anything at all without telling her everything.

'It's Mr Mystery . . . He's back in London, isn't he?'

'Yes, he's back, just for a little while. And I'm off next week. Penelope decided I needed a break. I know I've been a bit scatty lately and evidently it shows in my work.'

'You jammy old thing. How did you manage that one? You weren't going to tell me were you? You were just going to slope off somewhere and leave me wondering. So where are you off to? Somewhere glamorous?'

'Just seeing something of London. He doesn't know it very well so I'm going to show him round. Art galleries. Go to the theatre. Visit the Tower. You know, all the sort of things the tourists flock here to see. Penelope thought I needed a break so that's what I'm doing.'

'Unlike Penelope to grant any holiday without a full inquisition. So, this is all getting a bit serious is it?'

'I guess. Well, it's early days. But it will be good to have the time to get to know him a bit more.'

'Why don't we all meet up for a drink one night? Then we get to see your Mr Mystery.' Amanda shook her head.

'Sorry, But no. Not this time. I promise you'll meet him sometime soon.'

'You're really keeping this one close aren't you? What's so special about him?' Amanda blushed slightly but would say nothing. 'Okay, then what's wrong with him? Two heads? Aged ninety?'

'Nothing. Nothing at all. There's nothing wrong with him. I'll tell all when I'm good and ready.'

*　　　*　　　*

The week passed in a flash. They enjoyed being tourists and both felt very certain that this was the right thing for them both. Amanda pinched herself several times a day to make sure she wasn't dreaming. She kept looking at him as if she couldn't believe her luck. Again and again she asked herself, why me?

'I've never really spent time looking at painting before,' she said as they wandered round the National Gallery. 'There are so many wonderful paintings, it completely blows the mind.'

'I always plan to look at France's amazing galleries but somehow, there is always something else to do. Besides, it's so good not to have people recognising me all the time. I am known in France and so I don't have the same sort of freedom.'

'I've noticed people looking at you here. But I think that may just be because you are so worthy of being looked at.'

'Thank you but perhaps it is simply that they are jealous of me.'

Sometimes, he spoke lovingly of his home in Provence. She had never visited France, other than Paris, when she went on a school trip. Her experiences abroad largely consisted of regular trips to Spain to see her parents. They had moved there a few years ago, when she had left her own home to live in London. Though she missed them at first, it had its compensations. She always had somewhere warm to go for holidays and her own life had become filled with so many things since she began her job with *Personal*. She managed to talk to him about her parents and tell him something about her life here. But she was constantly on guard, wary of discussing anything connected with her work. She was too afraid of ruining everything to dare to say much. But he seemed happy enough to talk about his own life.

'Our vineyard is in a small village overlooking the Rhone Valley. It is very beautiful there and warm of course. The wine we make is mostly a rich red, typical of the area. Not dissimilar to Château Neuf du Pape. Most people have heard of that one.' He spoke of it all with such affection that Amanda wanted to be there.

'How did your parents meet?'

'My father was a wine buyer for a large company in Britain. My mother had taken over the business when my grandfather died. She was an only child and a girl at that, so she had to fight many prejudices. At that time, women in wine did not go down too well. But, they fell in love and pouf! that was it. They were married very quickly and my father had a new wife, a home and family and new job. He loves it there and never had any wish to return to England.'

'So, it runs in the family does it?'

'What do you mean?'

'Finding love in another country and getting married on impulse?'

'You don't regret it do you? You don't want to change your mind?'

'Of course not. I love you Sacha.'

'Et moi aussi. Je t'adore.'

'You make it sound so much more glamorous. I shall have to learn some French, if only to compete.'

'What do you want to do with the rest of today?'

'Let's go to the zoo. I haven't been since I was a kid. I just loved it then. Oh and there are the museums. Science and Natural History.'

'I vote for the zoo. We've done lots of things indoors and it's a nice day.'

56

'This has been such fun. I've lived in or near London for years and with you, I've seen things I'd never seen before. Maybe we all take the things that are nearby too much for granted. It's amazing how much we've been around and never seen anyone we know. Our secret has been kept safe.'

The week was ending and suddenly, it was the day before the wedding.

'Will your parents forgive you for not inviting them?' he asked.

'Probably not. My mother will be hurt that she didn't get the chance to make plans and buy a lovely big hat. But what about your parents?'

'They will feel the same. Do you mind? It will be a very simple affair. Just the two of us and probably unknown witnesses.'

'As long as it's you and me, I don't need anyone else. Except the registrar of course.'

'Then tomorrow it is. I still feel a little guilty not to give you the wedding of your dreams. I know that all girls want a church and a white dress. Flowers, friends and family making a big fuss.'

'When we tell everyone, we can have a party to celebrate. Our parents can all join together and share that if they want to.'

'That will certainly be some occasion.'

They collected the licence and checked on the booking for the following day. It was such a strange feeling to be facing possibly the

57

biggest event in her life without anyone knowing anything about it. Jenny would be terribly hurt. Probably never speak to her again.

'No regrets, my darling?' he asked as they were saying goodnight. 'Our last night of being apart.'

'Of course not. Well, sort of. You'll be travelling a lot, so there may be many nights of being apart. You're leaving again on Monday anyway, so we have only two more days and nights together.'

'I know. After this summer season, we can confess it all. The media can have their fun and I can show off my beautiful wife to the whole world.'

'I'm still not sure why it has to be so secret.'

'Fredo has worked to get me a sponsorship deal and the contract does not allow me to be married. Evidently, I'm less attractive to them if I have a wife.'

'I hope it doesn't spoil anything for you. But, secret it is. The most wonderful secret. I still can't believe you could love someone like me.'

'You are extraordinary. You are honest. Beautiful and not just wanting me because I may be rich and well known one day.'

Amanda blanched. He was totally wrong about her. She was a liar and had only met him in the first place because he was a minor celebrity. How he would despise her if he knew

58

the truth. She loved him far too much and dared not risk losing him.

'I want to marry you so very much, Sacha. I want to love you forever and ever and be your wife for always.'

'I promise to love you forever. Goodnight, ma cherie. A demain.'

'Till tomorrow.'

Alone in her flat, she pondered over her dilemma. Could she go through with this wedding with a lie as the only basis? How could she not? It was much too late now for confessions. She had her small suitcase ready packed. They were going to stay in a hotel for the weekend. Her new pale blue dress hung ready for the ceremony. Blue because Sacha had asked her to wear blue and to have her hair loose. She spoke to no one, not even her parents. There was no hen night. No great celebration. But that could all come later. Sacha had promised they would have a big party at the end of the season, when they could make it public.

*   *   *

Her taxi stopped outside the registry office just before ten o'clock. There he was. Waiting on the steps, holding a box. He was wearing a light grey suit and looking so perfect. She rushed up to greet him with a loving kiss. He gave her the box, containing a delicate orchid.

She felt tearful but his warm hug soon settled her nerves.

'I have asked for someone from the registry office to join us to be a witness. We couldn't ask anyone we know because . . .'

'It's all right. I know. As long as we are legal, nothing else matters.'

It was a blissful weekend and everything they both hoped marriage could be. In a lovely but discreet hotel, they had shared what they termed their honeymoon, though Sacha promised her a more exotic one after they announced their marriage.

'I almost feel as if it was a honeymoon sharing so many outings this week. But this has been truly wonderful, Sacha. Thank you.'

'I'm so lucky to have such a beautiful wife.'

All too soon, it was Monday morning again and Monsieur and Madame Manon shared breakfast for the last time before he had to leave for France and more of his punishing training schedule. Somehow, he had managed to keep Fredo away from them without him knowing anything about the events of the week. Amanda packed her bag and decided to take it into the office. She could always claim she had been to stay with her parents when she faced the inquisitive Jenny.

'Au revoir, ma cherie. I'll call you later and tell you of my safe arrival. Don't worry. I shall not be away for long. Two weeks. Three at the most.'

'I shall miss you. It's been a wonderful week.'

'An even more wonderful weekend.' They kissed as her taxi arrived. He stood on the pavement watching as it drove off, his hand raised in farewell.

*　　　*　　　*

It was a dreamlike day. Once more it was impossible to concentrate and Amanda feared Penelope's wrath if she didn't perform to her usual standard. Somehow, the foolish gossip she was obliged to write seemed even more tawdry than usual. She made up her mind that she should look for another job as soon as possible. Not yet, however. She needed to keep working to try to make the days between Sacha's visits fly. How her life had changed. She had her shiny new wedding ring on a long chain round her neck and took peeks at it when she was certain nobody was watching.

'So, how was the holiday?' Jenny demanded as soon as she had time.

'Excellent. Did me good. I feel like a different person.' She smiled inwardly, knowing she was speaking the truth.

'And Mystery Man? How's he? Where's he?'

'He's gone away again on business. Now, if I don't pull this article together, I shall be in deep trouble.'

'Poor Amanda. Trust you to find a perfect

61

bloke, I assume he's perfect? Only to find he's a frequent flyer. Well, not to worry. We'll get ourselves out somewhere exciting tonight and see what we can find to cheer you up.'

'Forget it. I have endless catching up to do at home. Washing, cleaning, work. I did nothing most of last week so I need to come down to earth and get back to normal.'

It was a hard decision, she decided when she finally returned home that evening. She looked around, thinking how small it was. Sacha hadn't even visited it last week so he had no idea of her simple lifestyle. She felt uncertain about everything now. The rush and excitement of the wedding and the bliss of being with Sacha had allowed her to forget about the next stage in their relationship. It was a terrible anti-climax. Somehow, she still had to confess about her real job. Unless she could give it up and find something else very quickly. But that would be impossible in so short a time. Finding a new job in the magazine world was never easy and it was really all she knew. Her phone rang and she saw his name on the screen of the phone.

'Hello? Sacha? I hope you had a good journey.'

'I'm missing you so much. I need to touch your hair again. To kiss you. To be with you. This is going to be much more difficult than I ever believed. I think you may have to come over to join me in France. Can you come at the weekend? I can't come back yet. There's a tournament Fredo has entered me for.'

'But won't that be too obvious if I turn up in Paris? I mean how will you explain me to Fredo?'

'We can spend Saturday together. I have to practise on Sunday. Please say you will come.'

'We've only been apart for one day.'

'I know. It's dreadful. I hope you're missing me as much as I miss you.'

'Of course I am. I'll see if I can make it to Paris. I can come on the Euro Star on Friday night maybe.'

'I shall be waiting for you. In fact I'll book you a seat right away.'

'Thank you, Sacha. Not before six o'clock though. Speak again soon.'

He called her back a little later to say it was booked. This was going to be a difficult time to keep her secrets. Perhaps she should tell him the truth at the weekend. Whatever happened, they were so much in love that he must accept it. It was a risk but one she should take if their marriage was truly to be long term. They talked long into the night on the phone. It was something to hold on to. She had never known anyone else with whom she could talk for so long.

It was only the second time she had been to Paris and never before with someone who knew his way around.

'We have two nights in a little hotel near to

Notre Dame. It is a small place but discreet. Much nicer than my rented apartment, which is always shared with others. I hope you don't mind but I did not want to be seen in one of those fashionable places. I am better known in France than England.'

'Anywhere is fine with me as long as you are there.'

It was another wonderful time spent together. At the top of the Eiffel Tower, he pointed out city landmarks and some places she might like to visit on her own on Sunday morning before she left for home.

'It's so beautiful. The whole city like a map so far below us.' She turned and kissed him, thrilled by the place and his company. There was a flash as someone took a photograph. 'I hope that wasn't us they were filming.'

'I don't know. Perhaps it was just a picture of the view or something. Don't worry.'

That evening, he took her to a small restaurant full of students from the nearby Sorbonne University where they ate kebabs, listening to loud music.

'Great atmosphere,' she shouted above the noise. 'And great food.'

'One of my favourite places. A throw back to my student days.'

On Sunday morning, he left her after breakfast and once more they had to part. It had been such a short time for them to be together.

'I hope the effort of travelling here was worth it.'

'Of course it was. How could you doubt it? I'll see you soon again.'

'A bientôt.'

'A bientôt,' she repeated, wondering exactly what it meant. It sounded good and he looked so pleased that she was trying out the language.

This was clearly going to be a very difficult few weeks. Nor had there had been any opportunity to make her confession. Perhaps she might, after all, find another job with a less intrusive magazine before he came back to London again. Halfheartedly, she looked around one of the art galleries before leaving to catch her train back to London. At least the train was all much easier than having to fly backwards and forwards. But for how long would this travelling and secrecy have to go on? It was all too much, she thought, as her eyes were filling with tears.

CHAPTER FIVE

Anti-climax was depressing her like crazy at the start of the next week. A couple of days later, Jenny dragged her out to lunch, refusing to take no for an answer.

'Right now, Amanda. You're going to tell

65

me the truth. You went to Paris at the weekend. Why do you look so miserable now? How exciting and why did you go? And what's more, how could you go there without telling me? That's such a mega thing to have done. I thought I was supposed to be your best friend.'

'You are my best friend. But how on earth did you know about Paris?'

'You left a Euro Star ticket stub in the waste bin. So why does my so-called best friend keep something like that from me? It's mega news. Headline stuff.'

'I can't tell you. Not yet.'

'It's Mystery Man isn't it? He lives in Paris. Oh yes. I'm right.' She clapped her hands together gleefully. 'Amazing. And you went to see him didn't you?'

'This is a secret. Promise you won't tell anyone. I mean it Jen. Nobody.'

'But it's so romantic. You can't possibly keep something like this to yourself. Why would you?'

'I have to. You have to.'

'I don't see why. What's so special about you going to Paris with a bloke? Oh, I get it. You don't want anyone to know that little Miss Goody Two Shoes has finally succumbed to a man's charms.'

'No. It's all a private affair. Between me and . . . well him. It's really nobody else's business.'

'And where's the gossip writer in you? Gone by the sound of it. Gone. Caput. Oh my god, I get it. He's somebody famous isn't he? When did all this start? It's the tennis player you were sent out to stalk.'

'I didn't stalk him. That sounds terrible.'

'So I'm right. It's a tennis star. Who? Which one?'

'Nobody you'd know. You're even less of sporty soul than I am.'

'Oh Manda . . . this is so exciting. Bags I write up the story.'

'You mustn't. You can't. Promise me you won't even think of it. He hates gossip magazines. Hates the intrusion into his private life.' Jenny stared at her friend, her jaw dropping in horror.

'Oh, Amanda. He doesn't know what your job is. That's awful.'

'I'd have lost him right at the start if he knew. I love him too much to risk losing him.'

'But you can't keep pretending for ever.'

'I know. Every time I've got close to telling him, I've flunked it. But I really want to try and get a job somewhere else. Somewhere that doesn't deal in gossip and the sort of rubbish we're producing.'

'Pays the bills though, doesn't it? And you must admit, it can be a really fun job. You used to think so.'

'I know.' Her woeful face finally got to her friend. 'It's just that I've just realised how intrusive it is into people's lives.'

'Price you pay for getting into the limelight

in the first place.'

'But not everyone seeks out such attention. Lots of people just get caught up in publicity. Think of all the people whose lives have been ruined by tabloid attention and gossip magazines. Why are the public so keen to know all the details of someone's life? Don't they have lives of their own?'

'Maybe you're right but I'm not about to give up my job because of some sense of ethical correctness.'

'Fair enough. But you must promise me to keep my news to yourself.' She wrapped her arms round herself and grinned. 'I love him so much. I still can't believe that someone like him can love me.'

'Nonsense. You're gorgeous and he's lucky to have you. It's okay, love. I won't say anything. Course I won't. But you do realise that this is probably the hottest story of the year? Do you think he's really as serious about you as you are about him? Has he said anything about a long term thing?' Amanda looked away. She was blushing furiously and knew she couldn't look her friend in the eye. Her hand went towards the chain and her wedding ring hidden away beneath her clothes. 'He has hasn't he? More juicy gossip. It's all too much to keep to myself.'

'Yes, it's a forever thing. But I can't say any more. Really I can't.'

'Oh it's just wonderful. I'm happy for you. I

really hope it works out. And I can't wait to find out who he is. You sure you can't even hint a bit?'

'No. We'd better get back or Penelope will be after our blood. We haven't got any excuse to stay out. Unless you've spotted some person who's famous for being famous?'

*   *   *

For the next two weeks, Amanda had to rely on calls and texts to keep in touch with her beloved Sacha. She'd given up thinking of him as her real husband as it made everything just too difficult with everyone around her. When they did speak, he was completely wound up in his preparations for the next tournament and had made no more suggestions for secret trips to Paris. She tried not to mind too much as she had always known this was how it would be for a while. Two more weeks and he would be back before the major tournaments in England. He needed two more significant wins in minor tournaments to make it through the qualifying rounds for the majors.

'Wish they made patience pills,' she told him one evening. 'I'd swallow a bucket load of them.'

'Not much longer my darling. I promise.'

*   *   *

Out of the blue, her world began to fall apart the next week. When she arrived at work, there was a sudden silence. She looked around for Jenny, to see what was going on but she was missing from her desk.

'Something happening?' she asked no one in particular.

'No, nothing.' The buzz began again and Amanda settled down at her computer. Unusually, there was an email from Sacha. He normally hated them but for once he had written very early that morning to her home email address. She usually waited to check her own email account from the office computer and was amazed to find it there.

Darling . . . I'm afraid I have some bad news. Remember the photograph at the top of the Eiffel Tower? They were picturing us. It's appeared in one of the newspapers here. Headline reads 'Who is the mystery woman with our own Sacha Manon?' They claim I am having an affair with some young woman and ask how this will affect my concentration for the coming tournaments. I don't think you could have been recognised but be prepared for some unwelcome attention. I have Fredo on the case already and he is denying everything.

Her face white, Amanda felt sick. Knowing how her colleagues managed to ferret out information, it wouldn't be long before the news broke here. The truth about her own job would be known and Sacha would hate her.

'What's up?' Jenny asked, seeing her friend looking quite ill.

'Bit of a problem. It'll get sorted but it's come as a shock.'

'If you're sure. Can I get you a coffee?'

'Thanks. That would be good.'

Amanda decided to trawl through the morning papers, as they usually did, on the scout for any stories they could follow up. With the tennis stars beginning to come into town, there might be something about Sacha and his new lady. She could find nothing but she was aware that she still being stared at by some of the other girls.

'Jen, do you know why I'm suddenly the object of so many people's interest today?'

'I'll find out. Here, enjoy.' She dumped a cup of coffee beside her friend and went to chat to the other journalists. If anyone could ferret out the truth, Jenny could. Sometime later, she came back and sat on the desk. 'Prepare yourself for a shock. Your secret's out. Someone emailed May with the gossip from Paris. There's a picture in one of the papers showing Sacha Manon and yes, you. Deep in a clinch but obviously both of you are recognisable. I confirmed that you had been in Paris but I promise, I said nothing else.'

'Oh no. I'm shot. How on earth can I keep it from the magazine?'

'You can't, Hon. May is already working on

71

the story. Penelope is going to be furious that you kept something this important to yourself. Especially when she knows you met him when you were actually supposed to be on an assignment. She will not be at all sympathetic to any soppy love story. Sorry, I didn't mean to be rude. I know you're not soppy really. But you're supposed to be totally immune yourself.'

'Oh what a mess. How on earth do I get out of this one?'

'Maybe you need to get to Paris as soon as you can and try to explain it to him. Otherwise, any thoughts of wedding bells have gone.'

'Actually, it's worse than that. We got married when I was off work.'

'Married?' Jenny almost yelled. 'And you never told me?'

'Quiet, you idiot.' May rushed over with her notebook.

'So it's true? Wow, that's hot. Lucky you. He's just gorgeous. Come on, dish the dirt. What's he like? Does he do any chores or is he the typical macho male? We need pictures. Together if possible. If he's still away, you'll have to have some taken on your own. Wow, this is the best. He's considered to be one of the up and coming stars.'

'I'm begging you, please don't do this. You'll ruin everything for me. For us. Find some other poor soul who's better equipped to deal with this nonsense. I never wanted to be a celebrity or famous in any way. I even turned down a by-line in the magazine so my real name wasn't known.'

'Sorry Amanda. Penelope would never forgive me if I let this one slip by. Especially with Queens and Wimbledon coming up so soon. Tennis is going to be *the* big news for the next issue and this is the biggest. Right on our own doorstep.'

Amanda closed her eyes, wishing herself anywhere but here. The room was swirling round her and she thought she might faint at any moment. How could she have been so stupid as to think she could keep it secret, when she worked in such an environment? It was a total gossip factory. She vowed never to write another story about any celebs who didn't want their lives set out on a plate for the world to see. Why should anyone be interested in her? Only it wasn't her, it was Sacha they wanted.

'I'm going home,' she whispered to Jenny. 'I have to warn Sacha and somehow, extricate myself from the headlines.'

But her plans were thwarted. As May came out of Penelope's office with a smug look on her face, the Editor saw her moving towards the door. She beckoned Amanda into her office and there began one of the most difficult interviews of her life.

Details of how they had met were demanded and she was well and truly scolded

73

for being unprofessional. 'Think it through Amanda. Do you want some affair with a man or do you want to continue a very promising career?'

'It's more than some affair. We love each other.'

Penelope sniggered. 'Oh yes, and for how long do you think you keep him happy? Love? Nonsense. No such thing. You may think he's in love with you but it will never last. Don't you know how many of these well known people have a string of girls chasing them? One each night. Course you know. We make it our business to know. Don't put yourself in that position.'

Amanda wanted to slap her face. What did this cold fish know about love? She was dedicated to her own career and probably had never shown interest in anyone on a personal level. She nearly blurted out the truth about their marriage but she knew it would be even more damaging to them both.

'I'm going to take some time out of the office today. I can't bear everyone staring at me. I'll work from home. If you'll excuse me.'

Penelope waved an impatient hand at her, dismissing her from the office.

*　　　*　　　*

Sitting in front of her laptop at home, she pondered over the words she could find to explain things to Sacha. She was tempted to rush off to Paris to explain in person but she knew that was not the right way.

My darling, she wrote. You were right. *One of the magazines has got the story and they plan to publish it in the next edition. I haven't said anything at all to anyone but it seems they know enough to publish an article. Speak later. I'm working at home today so call me when you can.*

It seemed little enough to write but she would explain things properly on the phone when he called. It was just before lunch time when he called.

'How are you?' he asked.

'Angry. Upset. I don't like this publicity. I promise, I haven't told anyone about us being married.'

'I'm coming over tonight, after I finish training. I shall come to your apartment, if that's okay. No reason not to as we are married and it's all above board. I expect the world will talk whatever we do or don't do.'

'It will be wonderful to see you. I shall look forward to it.'

'I'm not at all happy about it. I hope we can sort out something.'

He put the phone down without a single word of love. He was clearly angry and she dreaded seeing him instead of longing to see him. Listlessly, she dragged herself to the shops to buy ingredients to make supper. She wasn't much of a cook so it had to be

75

something simple. She bought fresh fish, salad, some crusty bread and a bottle of Sauvignon Blanc. She knew it would be something he would like, though in reality, she felt neither of them would be eating much. She still felt sick to the stomach.

It was almost nine o'clock when he called from a taxi to say he would be arriving in a few minutes. She turned on the grill and put the salad into a bowl. She lit candles and hoped the soft lighting would provide a gentler atmosphere than she was anticipating.

Looking weary and slightly more ruffled than usual, he came into her flat. He held out his arms to her and pulled her close. Almost disbelieving, she allowed herself to kiss him with the usual passion.

'I am so sorry, cherie. We should have been more careful. That person taking a photograph was no innocent. They recognised me and sold the picture to one of the cheap tabloid papers. And now, you say the news has reached England too. I fear there is nothing we can do. I threatened to sue the newspaper but they say we have no grounds for success. We were together. We did kiss in public for anyone to see.'

'I'm sorry too. It may be worse than you think. But, you must be hungry. I have prepared a simple supper. Nothing much.'

'Thank you. I think we both may need one of your double chocolate muffins to follow.

This is the first time I have seen where you live. It's not very big, is it?'

'London is very expensive, as you must know. This is the best I can afford. Here, sit on this chair. I'll pour some wine.' She felt suddenly shy. His large frame seemed to fill the room and she was slightly embarrassed by the modest place she called home. As she grilled the fish, she told herself, one more night. I must have one more night before I tell him the truth. His anger was not yet directed at her but it soon would be. Once he knew the truth, everything would end.

'Perhaps, after all we shall have to confess the truth to the world. If the press are spending their time guessing, giving them the truth may be better. Perhaps if we give one interview they will leave us alone.' She was clutching at straws.

'I can't tell you how much I hate all this intrusion. I have never looked for publicity. I just want to play excellent tennis and be famous only for being a good player. What I do in private is my own business. Oh, let's try to forget it for one more night. I have missed you so much.' He held out his arms to welcome her and she cherished the moment. It could be her last moment of happiness with this wonderful man, once he knew the whole truth.

*   *   *

Sacha slept surprisingly well, having been totally exhausted when he arrived. Amanda slept fitfully, feeling uncomfortable, as well as extremely worried about facing the coming day. She wasn't going to work at the office as she needed to spend the day on this most difficult confession. Leaving him sleeping, she went to make coffee and switched on her laptop. In deference to her position on the magazine, she had been sent a proof copy of the article. With growing horror, she read the text. One sentence hit her.

Our own column writer, Amanda Derry (known to you all as A-Jay) has herself hit the celebrity jackpot. She's been having a secret romance with the gorgeous Sacha Manon, rising tennis star. He was voted as the 'hunk we'd all most like to be seen with' by all our female office staff. Lucky Amanda. Will there be wedding bells soon?

The article went on with tenuous claims, most of which had been found in numerous, unlikely places. Once he saw this, Sacha would have the whole truth hitting him in the face. She read on, torturing herself with thoughts of the coming revelation. She didn't hear him coming to stand behind her and too late, she realised that he was also reading the text. As he drew breath, she jumped and closed the file.

'No point hiding it. I already saw the piece

78

you were working on. How could you? Amanda, how could you? One of the reasons I fell in love with you was for your honesty, for being open and straight forward. You must have lied to me so many times. Selling magazines? A blatant lie. You work for the very sort of magazine I hate most. I am sure you only became close to me because of your filthy magazine.' He muttered at length in French, none of which Amanda could understand but yet she knew exactly what he was saying.

'Sacha, it isn't true. I didn't cultivate you for a story. I do truly love you and when you asked me to marry you, I said yes because it was everything I could have ever have dreamed about.'

'So why were you waiting outside the tennis courts that day? An accident?' She looked down at her fingers, blushing and trying to think of something she could say to make things better. 'Say nothing. I want no more lies. It is perfectly clear that you were there to create some sort of story. Come for a drink you said. So sweet and innocent. But you wanted a story. Pure and simple. Do you even know the meaning of the word love?'

'Once we had spoken, I knew I could never write a story about you. I fell in love with you instantly. Everything about you was a dream. I promise, I told nobody. I kept our secret. Surely you must believe me? I didn't even ask my very best friend to our wedding for goodness sake. I haven't even told my parents. Sacha, I love you so much.' She tried to put her arms round him but he pushed her away.

'I don't want to even look at you again. I'll pack my things and go right now. I'll speak to my lawyers and have this mockery of a marriage annulled immediately. I can see that you wrote this piece yourself. It's on your laptop and you were working on it this morning. Clearly, that's why you were up before me. I see you wanted to get it in first before the news broke in the bigger papers.'

'I didn't Sacha. I would never do that.'

'But you are a professional journalist. We met because you came to me looking for a story. You are very professional. I never even suspected you then. How far would you really have gone to make some story out of this, had I not been so foolish as to trust you?'

'How can I prove to you that I do truly love you? I would never have married you if I didn't love you.' Tears were coursing down her cheeks. She was almost begging him to believe her words but he wasn't listening.

'I cannot believe anything you say now. This is all happening at the worst possible time for me. I am playing at Queens in a week or so. My first match is on the Monday. Opening day. I have to concentrate as best I can. Please make sure I don't have to see you again.'

As the room began to spin around her,

Amanda lay back on her sofa. She discovered that she couldn't stand up. She couldn't speak, as the love of her life tossed his belongings into his bag. Without a backward glance, he stormed out of her flat and out of her life. She lay still for a long time, knowing that she would collapse if she tried to stand. Her mind whirled round the events of the past weeks. She should never have allowed herself to become so involved with him. Never should she have agreed to marry him without confessing the truth. But if she had, she would have missed so many wonderful moments. He was hers and everyone else's dream. She had never fully believed that someone so gorgeous could actually be in love with her. The phone rang and she got up slowly, praying that it was Sacha.

'Amanda, are you all right? Only I was worried when you didn't appear at work again.' It was Jenny.

'No. I'm not all right. I never will be again. Sacha has left me. Thanks so much to all of you. My life is over. Grateful thanks to May for sending me her article. Sacha believed I'd written it and he never wants to see me again.'

'I'm coming over. Stay where you are.'

'No, I don't want to see anyone. Especially anyone from that blasted magazine. *Personal?* It's a word I don't want to hear again.' She put the phone down and lay back again. She felt sick and got up to fetch some water. The sink

81

was still full of last night's washing up. She'd imagined they might be finishing it off together after a cozy breakfast, not that it was very likely. She'd always known confession time was waiting round the corner. At last, the tears came. She wept as never before, totally wrapped in her own misery. The ring of the doorbell finally roused her. She asked who it was before opening the door.

'It's me. I was worried.' She opened it to see her friend standing with a paper mug of coffee.

'I was hardly going to leave you here alone. Here, coffee. Your favourite, with extra chocolate sprinkles. I got it from the little place along the street. Gosh you look terrible.'

'Thanks Jen. You know, this time, everything's way beyond chocolate.'

CHAPTER SIX

Jenny stayed with her friend for the rest of the day. Together, they washed up the supper things with Amanda weeping as she did so.

'I don't care what Penelope says. For once, I'm ignoring the demands of the office and the magazine. You're right. We do peddle people's privacy and nobody really cares what it does to their lives.'

'But as you say, it does pay the bills. Somehow, I have to get myself back onto the market. I'm on my own again and I have to earn a living. I suppose there's no way we can stop the article?'

'I don't think so. Besides, there will only be a queue of people outside trying to write another version. I think you need to dress up in your best. Put your make up on and let's go back to the office tomorrow, head held high.'

'I can't possibly. Thanks for the suggestion but I can't.'

It took two days before Amanda felt able to return to work. She took her friend's advice. Put on her make up, a smart suit and went into the office, head held high. There were one or two sympathetic glances but everyone was working as normal and nobody mentioned her story. Penelope called her into the office.

'I gather things haven't gone well for you?' she said, surprisingly amicable. 'While I can feel sorry for your emotional state, I need to know that you are still capable of producing some decent articles. A pity you didn't obey the rules and not become involved with one of our target subjects. Doesn't do to allow sentiment to become part of our game. One cannot afford a conscience. You still have a lot to give so I hope this can all be put behind us. Now, off you go and see what you find on the new young starlets who are coming in for the next premier.' She waved a dismissive hand and Amanda turned to leave. She was about to ask for a reference but thought better of it.

While she had work, she should keep it.

She tried hard to stay busy and when the weekend arrived, she filled her time with things to do. Her mind never stopped grieving for her lost love but somehow, she kept herself going. The days did drag but she was starting to fight back. She kept telling herself to fight back and from the outside, it certainly looked to everyone as if she got her fighting spirit back.

'I'm an independent woman,' she kept saying whenever tears threatened. When she saw the play list for the opening day of Queens, she couldn't stop herself from going to watch Sacha's match. Wearing a large straw hat and sunglasses, and sitting near the back of the court she hoped she would not be recognised. It was a lack lustre match and Sacha never stood a chance. As he was leaving the court, he glanced up at her and shook his fist. Her disguise had failed to work. Several people looked around and she slunk out of her seat hoping to get away before anyone else recognised her. She almost ran to the exit but she was stopped by a middle aged but handsome man, who looked in very good shape.

'How dare you ruin his career?'

'What?' She gasped.

'Your affair with my most promising player has totally ruined his chances.' The man had a heavy French accent and was clearly very upset. She realised that he must be the famous Fredo, Sacha's coach and self-appointed guard dog.

'I take it you must be Fredo.'

The man nodded.

'I'm sorry but you must have realised that it was never one sided. I never asked him to fall in love with me. I certainly never forced him into anything. It just happened.'

'He could not afford the distraction of a relationship of any kind. He is a good player but he needs to work harder than some of them. You saw what happened today. I had hoped that making the affair public would stop it all. But no, you turned out to be the very source of the publicity he could least need. You actually work on that dreadful scandal sheet. Did you deliberately set out to ruin his career? You are still well on the way to doing so. Leave him alone now and still it may not be too late. Always I have to try to protect him from such as you.'

'It was you who sent the message to my colleague, wasn't it?'

'How was I to know that you worked for that . . . that magazine? Sacré bleu! You are even worse than I could have believed. It is completely your responsibility that he lost today. Your fault, you dreadful woman. Why did you have to come here? Pushing yourself right in his face.'

'I was very discreet. I hid myself at the back

of the stand and I certainly don't see why I should take the blame. I did not tell him I was coming here. In fact I wish I hadn't come at all. You have certainly got your wish. Our affair, as you call it, is over. It's a pity he didn't concentrate on his tennis a little more today.' She walked away, leaving the Frenchman staring angrily after her. She hailed a taxi outside the courts, knowing she dare not stay any longer and run the risk of seeing her beloved Sacha, however much she would have loved to see him again.

I could always write an article myself, she thought. *I can tell the true story. All of it. And all about what has happened. How his supposed friend has dealt with his private life. That will show these scandal mongers what they do to people. That'll show him what I truly could have been doing had I wanted to. Had I really done what he believes I did.*

But she knew she couldn't do it. However hurt she felt, she would never be so vindictive.

It was a long week. She tried hard to work but seemed to be feeling perpetually sick and her mind was rushing off in all directions. Even her favourite coffee was tasting foul. Jenny suggested she should see her doctor and get something to help with her depression. She took the advice and made an appointment for the next day.

'Have you considered that you might be pregnant?' the doctor asked.

'Pregnant? No of course I'm not pregnant.'

'I think we should at least eliminate the possibility. I don't want to prescribe anything for you, just in case. Here, take this and pop along to the toilet to collect a sample. Then come back to see me and we'll do the test.'

Then began the longest few minutes of her life. She sat waiting for the result, thinking all the time, No. It wasn't possible. But it was . . .

'You are pregnant,' the doctor stated in a matter-of-fact manner. 'Can you remember the date of your last period?' Amanda counted back on her fingers. She took out her diary and looked back. It was hard to remember any details.

'I think it must have been at least six weeks. There's been so much happening in my life, I hadn't realised.'

'I take it there isn't a Mr Derry on the scene?'

'Actually, I am married but we've separated.' She swallowed hard so she didn't break down. 'I kept my maiden name for business,' she lied. She simply hadn't got round to changing it. Now it seemed pointless. 'I shall revert to my maiden name anyway.'

'We'll know timing better later, when you have your first scan. But from what you say, it looks like being a Christmas baby.'

She was in total shock. Sitting in her flat that evening, she began to think of the implications. A baby? She was having a baby.

Her parents would be shocked. Horrified in fact.

How would she be able to cope with working? She usually worked quite erratic hours. Though she was planning to look for another job, coming across one that paid well enough to care for herself and her baby would be a hard task. The girls at work would have mixed feelings too.

And Sacha? What on earth would he think? Would she even tell him? The way she felt right now, she would never tell him. Whether he had rights or not, it was irrelevant. He had clearly stated that he didn't want to see her, not ever again. He really hated her and all she stood for. No, telling him was quite out of the question. He would hardly want to see a child of hers, even if it was half his.

The tears threatened once more. She must snap out of it. No more tears would be allowed. She had responsibilities and needed to start planning. She switched on her laptop and began to look things up. She found out about pregnancy, what to expect and then she read a number of articles on working mothers and how they coped.

'I shall keep a diary,' she announced to the empty flat. 'I can turn it into a series of articles and relate it to other stuff I've done. If *Personal* don't want it, I'm sure somebody will.' Feeling cheered, she began her self-imposed tasks.

*   *   *

After five months of pregnancy, she was feeling very much better. In fact, she was feeling great. The sickness had passed quite quickly and she hadn't grown too large. With careful dressing, she was able to keep her secret from the others at work. Nobody had noticed that she had given up drinking alcohol, not even Jenny. Though her broken heart had done little in the way to heal itself, she had managed to put on a brave front. They were sharing lunch as usual one day, when Jenny stared at her.

'You've put on weight. Not a criticism and it quite suits you but it's not like you. I always envied the fact that however many muffins you ate, you never put on a pound.'

'I suppose I have put on a bit. Maybe I need to think about a diet.' Jenny made no reply and continued to stare.

'Know what? I think you're pregnant. Have you done a test?'

'Okay. Yes, I have but it's still got to stay a secret. I don't want Penelope pushing me out of a job.'

'She can't. If she fires you, you can sue. But what a thing. I assume you're keeping it?' Amanda nodded. 'Yes, obviously you are. If you're showing it must be too late. So, when's it due?'

89

'I've got something over three more months to go. I must have conceived at the beginning of everything—when we were first married.'

'And you've kept it to yourself all this time. Not for much longer though. So, it must be due around Christmas? Just after, maybe. What does Sacha think of all of this?'

'He doesn't know. It's nothing to do with him. Not now.'

'You haven't told him? Surely, it's got everything to do with him?'

'I don't think so. In fact, we might even be divorced by now, though I suppose I would have heard. In fact, I've heard absolutely nothing from him or about him. He may even have given up tennis for all I know.'

'But you can't keep this from him. Maybe he'll want to come back and he'll forgive you?'

'I'm not telling him. He was the one who left me. No, I have to manage on my own somehow or other.'

'But he has loads of money doesn't he? He will help you. You can't possibly manage on your own. Not look after a baby and work all the erratic hours we're expected to do. If you plan to stay in this job, of course.'

'Nonsense. Heaps of mothers are single parents and manage perfectly well. Though to be honest, I don't share your optimism that Penelope will keep me on. She'll simply make it too difficult for me to manage and make sure it's me who decides to leave. Saves paying redundancy. And since when did anyone in the company get maternity leave?' Jenny looked away. 'See? I'm right. Nobody. In tact Penelope sees pregnancy as a sort of disease. Something nasty that only idiots succumb to. Maybe she's right.'

* * *

By September, Amanda's pregnancy was quite obvious. Penelope had of course, noticed but had said nothing directly. She was biding her time. She did not make things easy and continued to send her favourite journalist out on assignments that were not at all suitable for a pregnant woman.

The tennis season was quiet and nothing much was going on in Britain so there had been no more gossip in the papers about Sacha Manon or indeed his lady friend.

Quite unexpectedly one evening, Amanda's phone rang.

'Amanda? It's me.' The voice was unmistakable. The sexy French accent and smooth tones made her heart leap right into orbit. As if it instinctively knew something, the baby began its usual evening gyrations.

'Sacha. Why are you calling me?'

'I missed you. I always have missed you. I want to see you again. Maybe we could make another start?'

'You said you never wanted to see me again.

91

Not ever. You said you were beginning divorce proceedings.'

'I couldn't do it. I was so very shocked at the time. The publicity seems to have died down now. I had a bad year on the courts. Fredo was always angry with me and we didn't work well together.'

'You do know it was Fredo who told the magazine about us? He thought if we split up you would concentrate on tennis and forget about me. About us.' Sacha was silent. 'Hello? Are you still there?'

'Yes. I'm still here. I did not know it was he who had told the world.'

'In fairness, he said he didn't know about my job. Where I worked. Or he said he didn't know. It was pure coincidence that he happened to contact my colleague. She was the one who recognised my picture.'

'Please, let us meet and talk. There may be a way we can be married properly again.'

She put her hand on her stomach and knew that this wonderful, brief fantasy was quite impossible. The last thing he could ever want was a baby taking up his life.

'I'm sorry but my answer is no. I daren't risk the hurt again. You broke my heart and I don't think I could survive it if happened again.'

'I'm offering to mend your heart. Please Amanda. Have dinner with me.'

'I'm sorry. Goodbye.' She put the phone down. She had never expected to hear his voice again and it had come as a total shock. She was still shaking. Once he saw her condition, he would immediately feel a sense of obligation. However he really felt about her, he would take simply pity on her. She did not want anyone's pity. However much she loved him, she did not want him to come back simply because he felt it was his duty. She and her baby would survive whatever happened.

His call had unsettled her completely. She had been coming to terms with everything and was making such progress. Now, after less than five minutes hearing his voice, she was back to resembling a wobbly jelly. She must be strong. She needed to continue with her plans and not let this interfere with the way she was running her life. All the same, she couldn't help speculating whether it might possibly work out. They knew so little of each other, beyond the intense passion that had enveloped them when they met and had led to all that had happened since. She had no idea what he thought about children. Would he love to have a child or hate the very idea? The baby kicked violently, letting her know he or she was alive and well. She made her decision. Seeing Sacha again was not an option.

When she came home from work the next evening, waiting on her doorstep was a huge bouquet of beautiful roses with a card that read, *Please let us meet again. My love, Sacha.*

'Oh Sacha If only.' But she knew she must

be strong.

'Did you get my flowers?' he asked in a phone call a little later. 'One for each night we spent together.'

'Please, you must stop this. You will be off round the world again at any moment. I can't cope with that sort of a life. I do still love you Sacha but I daren't see you again. I'm sorry.' She put the phone down and realised she hadn't even said thank you for the lovely roses. One for each night we spent together? She counted them. Not many for a supposed lifetime of a marriage. How romantic of him to know such a thing.

'Oh baby, your father is a true romantic but we can't be together. I wonder if you will ever know him?' Not for more than a few minutes at any time, was Sacha absent from her mind.

Later, there were more flowers and another call.

'I'm going back to France soon. Please see me. It will be some time before I am back in England again. There is nobody else for me.' Tearfully, she put the phone down on his pleas. He sounded so sincere but she was certain that if he saw her condition, he would run a mile. A rising tennis player needed full concentration. Fredo had told her in no uncertain terms, that if she stayed with Sacha, she would ruin his career. She left the phone off the hook for the rest of the evening, in case he tried again. She heard nothing more over the next few days. With mixed feelings, she assumed he had returned to France and that was the end of it.

CHAPTER SEVEN

Amanda was very late for work one morning. Jenny phoned her. 'Are you all right? Penelope is on the warpath. I said you were following up a lead at the airport. Inventive desperation eh?'

'I'm feeling terrible. I don't know what's wrong. Food poisoning maybe. I keep being sick and with this massive bump in front, I can hardly get over the bowl. I was going to call in but I . . . Sorry, gotta go.'

Jenny was worried. Something like this was not good for Amanda or the baby. She passed on the message to Penelope who looked furious.

'This pregnancy is taking over her life. Totally interfering with her work. She's no good to me if I can't rely on her. So what was this lead that she was following?'

'She didn't say. I expect it turned out to be nothing.'

Jenny went back to her desk and began working. Amanda's phone rang and continued to ring. She went over to it and picked it up.

'I have something to tell you. '

'Hang on a minute,' she interrupted. She immediately realised it had to be Sacha.

'No, you must listen to me. I am returning to France. I have given up playing tennis. Whatever I was dreaming about, it will not happen. I shall never rise above my current position. When I asked Fredo about his tip off to the magazine, he confessed all. I finished with him and without a coach and any incentive, there is no future in tennis for me. I know now that I am not good enough.

'I shall go back to my parents' home and I shall help them to make the beautiful wines of the South of France. This will be my new career. Thank you for listening to me this time. I shall not trouble you again. You have made it very clear that you do not want to see me again.' Jenny began to speak again but it was too late. He had hung up.

So, Jenny was thinking, the lovely Sacha has been in contact with Amanda again. Why on earth didn't she see him and tell him about his baby?

She found the display where calls were recorded on Amanda's phone, retrieved the number he had called from and put it away carefully. It must have been a mobile number she realised so he would most likely keep his phone with him. At least he hadn't been calling from a hotel somewhere. She might need to use it one day. Somehow, she had to get her stubborn friend back with this man she so clearly loved to bits.

*   *   *

The weeks passed all too quickly for Amanda. One Saturday in November she sat alone staring dejectedly through the window of her small flat. She gently stroked her swollen belly and sadly twisted the wedding ring from her finger.

'Hello baby,' she muttered, as she did at least once every hour or more. 'I'm trying very hard to do my best for you but it's so tough. Okay, I know it's all my fault that you won't have a daddy to love you but maybe I can love you enough for the two of us. Whatever the world says about me, I shall always know I did the right thing at the time. I love you, baby.'

She sighed deeply. There were still seven weeks to go before the birth and she needed to make her final plans. She wouldn't be able to work for much longer.

'This magazine job is much too stressful for you and baby,' the midwife had told her, as she neared her time. Besides, she felt distinctly unwell and needed some rest. Her Editor, the oh-so perfect Penelope Withenshaw, had been unsympathetic.

'Of course you're entitled to maternity leave, darling,' she'd said in a tone that had disapproval dripping from it. 'Just make sure you're back in the fold preferably within days.

If you're to be of any use at all, you need to be able to whizz off anywhere at a moment's notice.'

'But Penelope,' she began.

'I don't have "but" in my vocabulary. Of course, if it's a problem . . .'

The woman had no heart. Or understanding. She who knew nothing about children. Not that Amanda knew much but the learning curve was steep and fast.

'I'll do my best to find adequate child care.'

'Adequate doesn't come close, darling. Get it sorted or I'll have to appoint one of the many dozens of girls just waiting in the wings.'

Where on earth would she find the sort of childcare that Penelope was demanding? Did it even exist and if it did, how could she afford it? Would she be happy with someone else bringing up her precious baby?

Her future as a single parent was beginning to look bleaker by the minute. Ingenuously, she had believed she would be able to work from home and send in her material from there. Penelope would not hear of it. Her Editor sat in her large air-conditioned office, immaculate as ever and quite implacable.

'You need to be here. On the ball. Ready to follow up leads and catch the celebs when and wherever they are. If you don't want to do the job . . .'

'Of course I want the job. I love it and you know I'm good at it.'

'Yes, I'll grant you that. You certainly have the knack of getting close and asking the right questions. But just lately, you're letting this . . . this pregnancy,' said with a hateful sneer, 'become the most important thing on your mind.'

Of course this baby was filling Amanda's mind, as well as her life.

Did Penelope totally live and breathe her magazine, *Personal*, Amanda wondered? It seemed to be the only family, lover, life she needed. Nobody had ever heard her speak of anything or anyone else in her life. Never seen without perfect makeup and elegant clothes, she was totally chic. Amanda felt positively frumpy, despite the most stylish maternity clothes she could lay her hands on. Her complexion and hair looked good she knew, but there still remained the ever increasing middle section.

By now, all the staff in the office had heard the full story. She had worked terribly hard to ensure that nobody wrote a further episode of her story in the magazine. Several of them had offered, suggesting that Sacha might hear about it and come back. They had even offered her a fee for her side of the story. She remained adamant and luckily, on this occasion, they had listened. Though professionally she had retained her maiden name, she had sometimes, allowed herself to think of her married name. She assumed that

Sacha had never gone ahead with his threats to divorce her. Could one be divorced without knowing? She doubted it.

Whether it was the strain of her situation or some other cause, Amanda's blood pressure rocketed and the midwife insisted she stopped working and take plenty of rest. Her loyal friend Jenny was a frequent visitor and spent as much of the weekend with her as she could spare. Together, they had shopped for the baby things she needed. They had found several second hand bargains for the larger items and decorated the tiny box room ready for the baby.

'I don't know how you think you can still manage to work. Have you ever spent time with a new baby? Do you know how long it takes to do even the simplest thing?' Jenny had a much younger sister and had been fully aware of the problems after she was born. 'Even going to the shop becomes a major expedition with all the stuff you have to take.'

'I'll manage,' Amanda said through gritted teeth. 'Maybe I can sell some articles to other magazines. Go freelance or something. Work from home.'

'I'm going to cook something for you then I really have to go. I've got a couple of assignments that need completing before Monday.'

'I can manage. You go off. Thanks very much for coming round. I can easily heat up some soup.'

'Nonsense. You need proper nourishment. You look totally wiped out.'

Amanda lay back on her sofa. Jenny was right. She felt totally wiped out. She nibbled away at the omelette that her friend had provided but she didn't feel like eating. Only to herself could she admit that she just wanted the whole business over with.

'Oh Sacha, have I been selfish in not letting you share this?' she murmured. How much she would have loved to see him just once more. Just looking at his photograph made her loneliness so much worse.

CHAPTER EIGHT

With a whole raft of emotions running through her mind, Jenny dialled the number she had saved so many weeks ago. Her fingers trembled as she dialled. Amanda would be furious if she knew but she felt that it was the only thing to do. Sacha had the right to know he was about to become a father and her friend seriously needed help. She was unwell, depressed and if she wasn't coping at this point, she certainly wouldn't manage after the birth. She was due in a couple of weeks and there was little time left for everything to be sorted out.

The phone was answered. It was a woman who spoke rapid French. Jenny tried hard to remember just a glimmer of French from her school days but she had always failed miserably at languages.

'S'il vous plait,' she managed. 'Je needs to speak . . . to parler . . . to Sacha.' She spoke very loudly and slowly as if that could make up for her lack of language.

'Non. Pas possible.'

'But it's urgent. Are you his mother?' Heavens, she thought, perhaps it's a new girl friend or something. After all, it was his mobile phone. 'If you are his mother, then you should know you are about to become a grandparent. Please ask him to call me. I am Jenny, a friend of Amanda's. My number is . . .' She gave her a string of digits, wondering if she was even being in any way understood.'

The woman at the other end switched off the phone. Jenny stared at the instrument in her own hand.

'That went well.' She could only try again at another time. She felt herself breathing hard with the anti-climax of it all. Maybe she was doing the wrong thing after all. This was a sign. Interfering was something she was often accused of by her own family. Perhaps this what was what she was being told. All day, she tormented herself with the thought that she should try again. Several times, she picked up the phone to dial but replaced it. Maybe the female who answered was a new lady in Sacha's life. Maybe she hadn't actually understood what Jenny had said. Her phone rang. She leapt on it.

'Hi Jen. You busy?'

'Oh, Amanda. No, not really. Are you all right?'

'Sort of. Just felt like speaking to another human being. Sorry, I'm just being a total wimp aren't I?'

'Course not. I'll come round after work. Maybe we could go to see a film. Take you out of yourself for a while. Rest up during the day and look to see what's on near you.'

'Thanks Jen but I'm not sure it's a good idea. Sorry, I shouldn't have disturbed you at work. How's everyone?'

'Fine. Penelope is her usual charming self. Better go. I'll see you later.' Amanda was clearly feeling down and needed cheering up. If she couldn't get hold of Sacha, then maybe she needed to organise something. Maybe a baby shower would be a good idea. She went into overdrive for the rest of the morning and got the other girls involved. Everyone agreed to buy something for the baby and they would all go round to Amanda's flat the next evening. Even Penelope agreed to make a contribution and offered to buy a few bottles of wine. Not exactly what a mum to be needs but the rest of them could enjoy a bit of a party. She dialled Sacha's number once more but there was no

103

reply. She had done her best. Half an hour later, her own phone rang.

'Hello? Someone from this number called me. I recognised the London number. Is that you Amanda?'

'Sacha? This is Jenny, Amanda's friend.'

'Is something wrong with Amanda? Did you call before? My mother took a call from England recently but she speaks little English. She only told me this morning when I said someone had again called my number.'

'Amanda is unwell. Look, this will be a shock. She is about to have a baby. Your baby, of course.'

'My baby?' He muttered something in French that was quite incomprehensible to Jenny. 'You mean I am going to be a father?'

'Yes, you are.'

'But when? It is many months since I was with ma chère Amanda.'

'It's due very soon. She's at home, feeling unwell and rather depressed.'

'But why did she not tell me this so important news? Does she hate me so very much?'

'She loves you Sacha. She didn't tell you about the baby because she was afraid that you would take pity on her. Feel obliged to help her. And then you might feel trapped into something you didn't want.'

'I was selfish. At the time we were together, I was so shocked that she didn't tell me the truth about her work. I thought at first that she was only using me for a story. I should have understood. I should have known that someone as open as she was, did truly love me. I have been so stupid. I have finished playing tennis. I stay at my parents' family home.'

'Yes, I know. You called Amanda's phone one day and I answered it. You didn't give me a chance to explain that I wasn't her.'

'And did you tell her that I had given up tennis?'

'I . . . well . . . no. I haven't told her. She was always too upset whenever your name was mentioned. She thought you may have divorced her without her knowing.'

'So why have you called me now?'

'Because I thought you should know. I thought you might want to see her again. You might even want to be a parent.'

There was a long silence. 'Sacha?'

'Yes. I am thinking. As you say it, is a big shock. I need some time to think. Amanda did not tell me herself so I have to decide if she really wants me to know. To be a part of her life and that of my child. Thank you Jenny. Look after her for me.'

Jenny now faced a new dilemma. Should she confess her interference or wait to see what happened? She decided to wait. No point in raising her friend's hopes. Or maybe incurring her friend's wrath? For now, she would concentrate on organising the baby shower. In fact, she began putting some notes together. This could even make a story, if things went well and Sacha came back. A few photographs taken at the time would not go amiss and Amanda might like to have a record of the occasion. She was becoming as bad as Penelope, Jenny decided.

It was hard to keep the secrets from Amanda that evening.

'What are you up to?' Amanda asked. 'You've got something going on, haven't you?' They had gone to the cinema after all and she felt better for the change of scene.

'One or two of the girls thought they might call round tomorrow after work. Is that okay?'

'I suppose so but I'm not much company at the moment.'

'You're right. You're a miserable old fogy and need cheering up. We'll be over around seven so make sure you're dressed in something other than that old dressing gown you inhabit most of the time.'

'Thanks Jen. You're a good mate.'

*   *   *

All the next day, Amanda rested. She knew she had to be ready for the girls and got herself showered and changed in good time. She tidied the flat and wondered if she ought to get some drinks and nibbles organised. But it was too late. Someone was already at the door. Jenny came in, laden with bags and boxes.

'What on earth?'

'It's a baby shower. We're having a party. Everyone's coming. Now, get the glasses out of this box and give them a wipe.'

'But I haven't got anything in. No food or anything.'

'Course you haven't. I've brought everything. Even Penelope coughed up for the booze and half the food. Come on. Get yourself into gear. They'll be here soon.' She opened a black sack and a forest of silver, pink and blue balloons floated out.

'Oh Jenny, what can I say? Did you know about this last night?'

'Course I did. That's why I warned you to get out of that scraggy old dressing gown. You look half decent tonight. Now, oven on please. There are various savouries to be warmed up.'

Within half an hour, eight of her old friends had arrived, all carrying parcels wrapped in pretty baby paper. Amanda was near to tears as she opened packages with trendy little outfits, suitable for a boy or girl. There was a basket of baby toilet products and several tiny stuffed toys. Someone had even brought a giant pack of disposable nappies, causing some hilarity.

'They are all so gorgeous, thank you.'

'Let's drink a toast to the safe arrival of the new little Derry.'

'Safe arrival of the new little Derry,' they said raising their glasses. Amanda downed her cranberry juice, thinking it might be nice to enjoy a glass of wine again.

There were many questions which she now felt able to answer truthfully. 'How could she get married so secretly and not tell anyone?' they wondered.

'It made it even more special somehow. Nobody knew anything, not even our parents. I suppose they never will.'

'Cheer up. You're soon going to have a gorgeous baby. Lucky you.'

'Suppose it isn't gorgeous. It might have my nose and I wouldn't wish that on anyone.'

'Rubbish, you're gorgeous and Sacha is an absolute dream on legs. I could take up watching tennis just to enjoy the view.'

'Oh, he's given up tennis,' Jenny blurted out without thinking.

'How on earth do you know that?' her friend demanded. Jenny blushed scarlet and looked very uncomfortable. She drew a deep breath, wondering if she could get away with a half truth.

'I answered your phone one day in the office. It was Sacha calling to tell you he was going back to France to work in his family vineyard. I couldn't get a single word in before he hung up again.'

'And you never told me?'

'There seemed little point. You'd never

mentioned to me that you'd ever spoken again and he was angry enough to think you didn't care.'

The silence that followed was difficult. She pulled herself together and said brightly,

'I'm sorry, please help yourselves to food and more drink. Come on everyone, this is a party. Do you think a tiny glass of that bubbly would harm me? Just to welcome junior here?'

She held out her glass and someone poured her a tiny helping. Seeing how weary she looked, the others began to clear up the plates and glasses and tidy away everything they could before they drifted off.

'Thank you all so very much. It's been a great fun evening and really good to see you and I love all the presents. It makes it all seem much more real now and I'm really thrilled to think my baby will have so many aunties.' They kissed her good night and wished her luck and eventually Jenny was left alone with her.

'I'm sorry I didn't tell you about Sacha going back to France. He said he knew he would never be good enough to win any major tournaments and he had split with his coach or something.'

'It doesn't matter.'

'Do you still want me to be your birth partner? I shall understand if you've changed your mind and would rather have someone else.'

'Of course I do Jenny. Who else could I

have? It's not so long now. You know, after tonight, I think I'm beginning to look forward to it, so much more. Thank you again for bringing everyone here. I think I needed the boost of friendship.'

*   *   *

As she alone lay in her bed, her mind was racing. She had been keeping secrets for so long it was a relief that she could tell people the truth. But there were still her parents who knew nothing of the massive events in her life this year.

They lived in Spain and she had simply avoided telling them anything and nor had she visited them. It was always easy to claim that she was too busy and never had enough time. They would be shocked to the core to find that she had married and that they were about to be grandparents.

She had decided to wait until after the birth. She tossed and turned, trying in vain to get comfortable. The ache in her back was awful. Her stomach felt tight and made her feel short of breath. She should never have had that sip of wine. She got up and walked around the flat. The first contraction struck her.

'Oh heavens. I shall never drink again.' The pain stopped only to be replaced some minutes later. Her brain suddenly clicked into gear. It was the baby coming. How could she have been so dense?

Quickly she dialled Jenny who promised she would come back immediately. She lived only a short distance away so it should be a matter of minutes. Her teaching from the ante-natal classes found its way back into her mind and she began to follow her instructions.

She put her bag into the hall and waited for Jenny. She would travel to the hospital in her car rather than call for an ambulance. Plenty of time. Hospital. She needed to call the hospital to tell them she was coming. But the next contraction began and she had to sit down for a moment. Where was Jenny?

She dialled the number she had written in large letters and left stuck above the phone.

'Hello? I think my baby's started to arrive. I shall be coming in soon.' She gave them all her details and then waited for her friend to arrive feeling a bit of a mixture of both apprehension and excitement.

'I'm here,' Jenny called. 'You might have let me have more than two hours sleep. Never mind. All in a good cause. All set?'

'You all right? You seem even more tense than I am.'

'I'm fine, thanks. I'm just realising this is such a big responsibility. I'm proud you asked me of course but I just hope I can do the job.'

*   *   *

When they arrived at the hospital, it all fell into place. She was examined by the midwife, who confirmed that she had certainly begun her labour but there was still a long way to go.

'Don't worry,' she said cheerfully. 'It often takes a long time for the first. Everything's fine.'

'You go to work if you want, Jen. I'm clearly going to be here for ever.' It was almost noon and she had made little progress. In fact, there had been times when everything seemed to have stopped and she was threatened with being sent home again. Jenny had argued that because Amanda lived alone, she should stay where she was. The staff agreed.

'Don't worry, I'm not leaving you. I shall see this through. Do you want anything? Food, drink?' She kept looking round at the door as if she was expecting someone.

'I'm fine. What are you looking for? You keep staring at the door.'

'Nothing. I keep thinking the staff will be back to check on you. I'm taking my responsibility seriously.

'Just wish junior would make an appearance. Oooh, here it goes again.' She walked round the room, breathing as she had been taught and waiting for the contraction to ease off. By evening, the medical staff had decided that they needed to help the baby make its appearance and prepared to take her into the delivery room. Jenny came with her, holding tightly on to her friend's hand.

'Okay Amanda. Try to relax.' The words were lost in the middle of another massive contraction. The door opened and Amanda gasped. Looking totally exhausted and quite distraught, Sacha rushed to her side and took her other hand.

'My darling. I came as fast as I could. Not for the world would I have missed this moment. Our first child is about to come into the world.'

'Sacha?' she managed to whisper through her tears. 'Am I dreaming? Have they given me something?'

'I am really here and no, you are not dreaming.' Nothing else mattered. The pain seemed to evaporate and very soon, her son was born.

'He was clearly waiting for his daddy to arrive,' the midwife said with a smile. 'No need for our intervention after all.'

'Thank you.' Jenny was highly emotional. 'Thank you for letting me share that moment. I shall never forget it.'

'And thank you for calling me. I also should have hated to miss the moment,' Sacha said.

'You called him? But wasn't it a terrible shock?'

'The shock, I was used to. Jenny had also called me last week to tell me the news. She said the baby was not expected for a couple more weeks. I made some preparations and I would have come sooner but I then couldn't get away. A crisis at home. Also my parents were very shocked. They did not know about our marriage and assumed this child might not be mine. They were not happy. But we can discuss all of that later. Let us enjoy meeting our new little son.'

Jenny slipped away and left them together, a family for the first time. The tiny boy, wrapped in a sheet, lay on his mother's tummy. They gazed at their tiny son with his fists clenched and eyes screwed up and closed. He opened them suddenly, a wide, misty blue gaze, apparently fixed on his father's face. He gripped the proffered fingers and the new parents laughed.

'He will certainly be able to hold a tennis racquet,' Sacha said. The midwife came back into the room.

'Excuse me but we need to take the baby for a little while. Some tests to be done and I'm sure you'd like to see him all nice and clean. And we need to make you more comfortable. If all is well, you can go home later today.'

'Really?' Sacha said, his eyes wide. 'So soon? How will we know what to do?'

'The health visitor will visit you to make sure all is well. Don't worry. You have a very healthy son.' She went away with the baby, leaving the new parents alone for the first time in many months.

'I shall never understand how you could

think that I wouldn't want to be a father.'

'We'd never spoken of having children and I thought your tennis career meant everything to you. Then I met Fredo and he told me I was ruining your life and spoiling your chances of success. When you discovered the true nature of my job, you were so very angry.

'Believe me, so many times I was going to confess all about it but I was too scared of spoiling the most wonderful thing that ever happened to me. I was right as it turned out. You hated me. After we broke up, I discovered I was pregnant and I knew it was up to me to cope with it. I could never allow you to feel obligated to me. To feel sorry for me or duty bound to be with me would be even worse. When you called me, I couldn't meet you and allow you to see me in this condition.

'I hope you understand what I am saying. If you were ever to love me again, it had to be because you wanted to and not because you felt you owed me something.'

'Oh Amanda, Amanda. So much confusion. So much misunderstanding. I know I was filled with fury that you could have misled me so greatly about your work. I thought that you had deliberately lied to me about it and I could no longer trust you about anything else. I am so sorry. What time we have wasted. I could have shared the waiting months with you.'

'So, do you really think our marriage might work?' she asked. He nodded, barely able to speak with his emotions running so high. She smiled happily. 'How long will you be able to stay with me now, assuming you want to of course?' He recovered himself.

'For as long as you like. Work in the vineyard is quiet at this time of year. Our workers will do any tasks that need doing. When you are recovered sufficiently, I'd hoped you would come back to France with me? I'd like us to make our home there. My parents' vineyard is in a beautiful place and we can have our own house. There is a place, a sort of barn I suppose it would be called, which we can easily convert. If that would please you, of course.'

'I really want us to be together, as a family. Of course I do. But this is all such a big change in my life. I don't even speak much French and I wouldn't have a job. How can I earn anything in another country when I don't speak the language?'

'I'm sure you'd soon learn, but my father is British so that could be a good start. I have a good career in wine making and we have no shortage of money. But I understand, you are used to being independent and want to pursue some career. You can work at home perhaps as a freelance? With emails and new technology, it doesn't really matter where you are based, does it?'

'It all sounds possible, but please don't rush me too much. Let us get used to being parents first. Remember, I was planning to be a single parent and now that is also changing. It takes some getting used to.'

*   *   *

They talked non-stop for the rest of the day.

There were so many plans to be made and so much catching up to do. During the times when the baby was awake they were fully occupied with him and feeding him.

Amanda had promised herself that she would feed him at first, until she managed to find childcare and go back to work at least. Now that was all changed, except the feeding routine she still had to come to terms with. She was full of questions while she had the professionals on hand, knowing that soon, they would have to cope alone.

It was evening before they left the hospital. Sacha was amazed at the speed of everything. They were kept in hospital for much longer in France, he assured her. Fortunately, she had prepared most things for the baby's arrival and the tiny crib was awaiting its new occupant.

'Are you sure it's warm enough for him? It's a very cold evening.'

'I left all the heating on when I left to go into hospital so I'm sure he will be just fine. I'm afraid that I haven't got very much in for us to eat. I wasn't expecting any of this to happen just yet.'

'What shall we do for Christmas?'

'Christmas?'

'It's in just five days. I don't suppose you will be ready to travel by then so we shall have it here. Just the three of us.'

'I hadn't realised it was so soon. But just us sounds great. And when are we going to have our belated wedding party?'

'Soon. Before we go to France. Then all your friends can meet our son. We must find a name for him. Have you thought of a name?'

'Not really. I like Michael or should we make it Michel?'

'Michel Manon. That sounds great. It will look good when it appears up on the board at Wimbledon.'

'Oh, so he's to be a tennis player is he?'

Their conversation went for much of the night, there was just so much lost time to be made up.

CHAPTER NINE

After a couple of days, Amanda phoned her parents to break the news to them. They were shocked, horrified and secretly very pleased that they had a grandson.

'Why ever didn't you tell us?' her mother demanded. 'We could have helped. You could have come to live with us here in Spain and

118

we'd have looked after you.'

'I didn't want to live in Spain. You know I didn't. However, we are probably going to live in France. At Sacha's family home.' Even without seeing her face to face Amanda could sense her mother's total disapproval, or was it perhaps, jealousy?

'We shall catch a flight as soon as we can. I hate Britain in the winter but this is a rather special occasion.'

'We're planning to have a sort of belated wedding party in January, so why not wait to come then?'

Sacha later congratulated her on her tact. He wanted and they both needed a quiet Christmas.

'Now I have to show similar skill in inviting my parents.' He telephoned his home in Provence.

Amanda listened to musical sounding fluent French as he chatted to his mother. She picked up the odd word such as Noël, joyeux, mon fils, and so on but most of it was completely over her head. It did give her some concern about the future. How could she live in a foreign country without speaking the language? Heavens, she may not even be able to speak to her own son if she didn't learn the language with him.

'My parents will also come over for our wedding party. Now all we have to do is to decide on a date and organise it.'

'That will have to wait for now. Our son is demanding food yet again. At this rate, I honestly think he's going to be even taller than his father, by the time he's six.'

*　　*　　*

Quite early on Christmas Eve, Jenny arrived unexpectedly but laden with gift-wrapped parcels and bags full of all manner of Christmas goodies.

'Oh Jenny, that's so kind of you. But now I feel terrible. I haven't even been near a shop and I haven't bought any gifts for any one. I thought I'd have plenty time to do that . . .'

'I thought you wouldn't. I've got a full feast here in this box. If Sacha wouldn't mind going down to my car, there's a tree and several other bits and pieces.'

'This is all too much. But thank you. You are the best friend anyone could want.'

'Don't mention it. Now, there's some Champagne somewhere, to toast the new arrival. Yes, here it is.'

They ate and drank some of the things that Jenny had provided and discussed the coming party.

'Don't know where we should hold it. Obviously, this place isn't nearly big enough.'

'Leave it to me. I've got an idea,' Jenny said. 'Except the husband among us might resist. I was actually thinking of the office. The big meeting room would be fine. Move out the big tables and it will be perfect.'

'What do you say Sacha? Could you cope with visiting such a dreadful den of iniquity?'

'As long as all the cameras are hidden away.'

'Oh but I shall want some pictures as a record of the occasion. Anyway, nobody will be interested in us as a story. Not now you've given up tennis and you're no longer a rising star.'

Jenny frowned. She knew it would still make a heart warming story but wisely, said nothing. She was already writing the headline in her mind. *Tennis Star Gives Up Everything For His Wife And Baby*. She stored it away for possible future use. She admired and cuddled Michel, approved his name and handed him back to his mother rather quickly when he did what babies do.

'Think he needs his mother,' she announced, pulling a face. 'Remind me never to have babies.'

'That's fine. He actually needs his father,' Amanda told her.

Her friend's jaw dropped.

'You mean, he actually changes nappies?'

'Certainly,' Sacha told her as he took charge and went off to make for the baby's room.

'Has this man got a brother? Drop dead gorgeous and a modern man to boot. I thought French guys were far too macho to be involved with all that messy side of things.'

121

'No way. He was partly responsible for creating this little boy, so he has to share most things. Except the feeding of course. Nature hasn't got that one sorted yet.'

She stayed for another hour, laughing and chatting. At last she stood up, ready to go.

'Now you love birds, I shall leave you alone. Enjoy Christmas. Pity me when you think of me wrapped up tight in the family home. Christmas dinner with all the family. Mum telling me I look too thin and stuffing me with extra roast potatoes to undo all the good dieting I've been doing for months.'

'Sounds great,' Sacha said, not a trifle wistfully. 'I've never experienced a British Christmas.'

'Totally overrated,' was the rejoinder. 'Too much anticipation and a total anti-climax when it arrives.' Jenny breezed out of the flat, leaving them feeling as if a whirlwind had just invaded their lives.

* * *

'She's amazing, exhausting and clearly a very good friend you have there. Now let us return to our peaceful life.'

'What do you think about a party at the office? It's nice and central for everyone and it is a lovely room.'

'If that's what you would like and would make you happy. Fine. So, when shall we have our party?'

They fixed on the second Saturday after New Year. People might still be in celebratory mood and there was just about time for the two lots of parents to fly over. Both of them felt slightly nervous about meeting their respective new in-laws and hoped that their parents would get on together. Jenny proved a tower of strength and had organised everything at the office. Even Penelope had entered the spirit of the occasion and provided the name and address of her favourite caterers.

'I never thought I'd be condoning a marriage celebration in my offices but I suppose this will be a different sort of occasion. I shall be sorry to lose you Amanda,' she had said when they had all visited to make the arrangements. The new mother had been mildly amused to see the expression of distaste on her boss's face when she had looked at Michel. The other girls had more than made up for it as they'd cooed over the new arrival.

*   *   *

Their parents arrived a couple of days before the party, so there had been time for the formalities of meeting together. They didn't need to have worried. Everyone got on famously right from the start.

'He's gorgeous, darling,' her mother said

123

immediately. 'And he clearly adores you and his baby. I just don't know why we didn't know all about him from the start. And his mother, so elegant and quite charming.'

Sacha's mother had made a great effort to speak in English and Amanda's fears of finding herself in difficulty when she moved to France, evaporated. The two sets of parents stayed in the same hotel and were soon chatting like old friends.

'See? As I told you, it will all be fine,' Sacha whispered to the mother of his child. 'My parents love you right away as I knew they would and your father and mine are already discussing the merits of French and Spanish wines, like a pair of real connoisseurs.'

'I am still amazed at the way you can flip between French and English without hesitating. I hope our son will learn to be bi-lingual too.'

'Of course he will. English will he be his mother tongue and I shall speak to him in French. Soon, he will translate for you any words you don't know.'

'It's all going to be wonderful isn't it? I'm so much looking forward to our life together.'

There was a great deal of joy in the room at the party a couple of days later. As she looked round at friends and family, Amanda knew she had made a good decision to marry her wonderful husband, all those months ago. Even Fredo had arrived with a smile on his face.

'I must give you some apology,' he said in his strong French accent. 'I did never dream that you and my boy could actually be married. I see now that it was a how you say, double agreement?'

'Mutual. I think you mean mutual attraction. I never intended to spoil his career, I promise you.'

'Perhaps he was never going to be a number one tennis player. Mais, alors, one always can have hope. I have a new protégé now. He is much less aged. I shall keep him apart from you magazine people.'

'You tried hard to keep us apart so don't have your hopes too high.'

'Are you going to introduce me?' Jenny asked as she came to join them.

'This is Fredo. Sacha's one time coach. Fredo, meet my very good friend Jenny. I shall leave you to get to know each other. Excuse me.'

She smiled to herself as she left them. It wouldn't take long for Jenny to get the name of his new protégé. She quite looked forward to seeing Fredo's picture on the front cover of *Personal*.

'Amanda dear,' Penelope said, when she finally got her alone. 'I trust you are going to allow us to publish just one small story about you and your lovely family. Then we might do a series . . . well you could write it yourself, a

125

series on how it feels to move to another country and the difficulties you might experience. I think our readers will love it. A real human interest story. Then you can keep your hand in and possibly stay on as our very own foreign correspondent. I think this could be very good for all of us. An insight into life in France itself.

'There must be many Brits living in your area. Famous ones too. Escaping from this depressing weather to warmer climes.'

'I'll have to discuss it with my husband. I simply don't know how he would feel about it. I somehow doubt that he will agree. But be assured I shall never ever try to keep anything from him in future. I've learned my lesson and nearly caused a complete disaster. Now, if you'll excuse me, I think my lovely new son might be needing me. He's been a bit too quiet for far too long.'

'Oh dear, what a waste of a promising talent. You've gone all domesticated.' Penelope's nose wrinkled in disgust.

'You can bet on it.' Amanda said happily, rushing away from most of her one-time ambitions.